The world is in peril.

An ancient evil is rising from beneath Erdas, and we need YOU to help stop it.

Claim your spirit animal and join the adventure now:

1. Go to scholastic.com/spiritanimals.

2. Log in to create your character and choose your own spirit animal.

3. Have your book ready and enter the code below to unlock the adventure.

Your code: NHRN74TTXJ

By the Four Fallen,
The Greencloaks

scholastic.com/spiritanimals

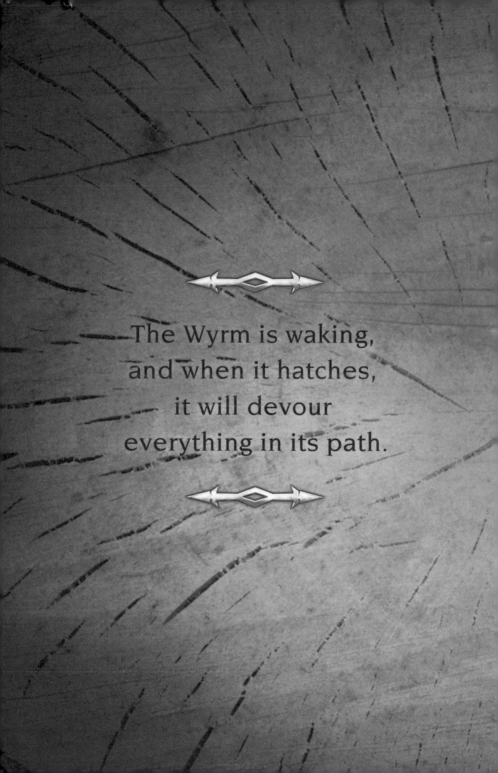

The Wyrm is waking,
and when it hatches,
it will devour
everything in its path.

THE BURNING TIDE

THE BURNING TIDE

Jonathan Auxier

SCHOLASTIC INC.

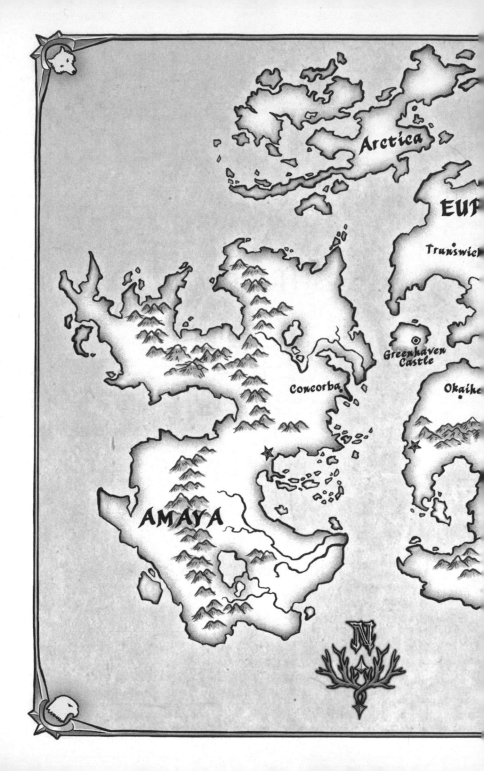

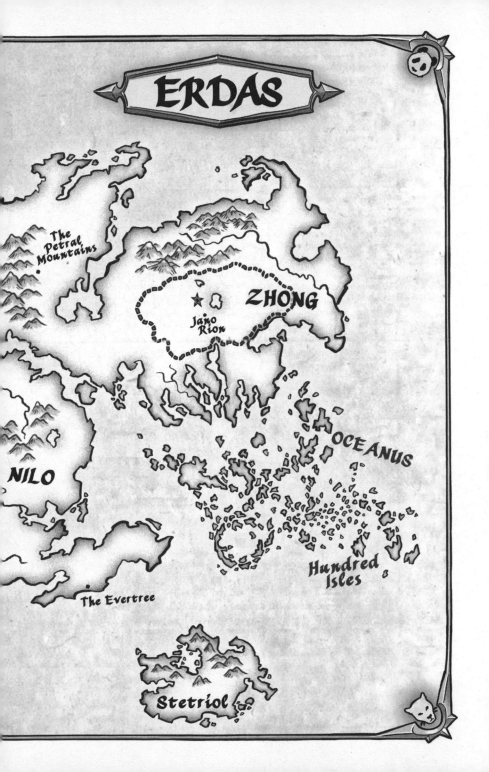

This book is a work of fiction. Names, characters, places, and
incidents are either the product of the author's imagination or are used
fictitiously, and any resemblance to actual persons, living or dead, business
establishments, events, or locales is entirely coincidental.

Library of Congress Control Number: 2016940992

ISBN 978-0-545-83214-4

10 9 8 7 6 5 4 3 2 1   16 17 18 19 20

Book design by Charice Silverman
First edition, September 2016

Printed in the U.S.A. 23

Scholastic US: 557 Broadway • New York, NY 10012
Scholastic Canada: 604 King Street West • Toronto, ON M5V 1E1
Scholastic New Zealand Limited: Private Bag 94407 • Greenmount, Manukau 2141
Scholastic UK Ltd.: Euston House • 24 Eversholt Street • London NW1 1DB

THE BURNING TIDE

FROM THE STARS

THE SKY WAS FALLING.

It had started seven moontides before. The elder ape of the tribe was about to commence the last feast when he spotted something in the heavens above—a small speck of light burning in the sky. But unlike the stars, this speck was moving straight toward Erdas.

This was long ago, back before Kovo even had a name.

He remembered his entire tribe stopping their eating to stare up through the dark canopy of trees, all of them thinking the same thing—

The sky was falling.

"What?" Kovo's mother had asked, signing the question with her black gorilla hands.

The elder ape had wrinkled his gray brow and gestured with his hands. "Do not know."

Concerned grunts moved through the tribe. It was the first time Kovo or anyone else had heard the elder ape say he did not know something. Usually such an admission would mean death—the other silverbacks in the tribe would have attacked, in order to take his place—but they, like Kovo, were transfixed by the light above.

Kovo knew their land was surrounded by a vast ocean of stars, which spun in their own paths. But even as the sky churned in its usual course, this burning piece broke the harmony, cutting a path in its own direction.

Every night Kovo's tribe gathered and watched the speck again, and every time it looked bigger and burned brighter. Soon they were able to see the speck even during the day. It became clear that this falling piece of sky was moving toward the land.

The other animals in the jungle knew of the sky falling too. Kovo had seen some boar herds in the lower brush congregating to watch the approaching speck. He heard the nervous chatter of the falcons in the east as they circled the sky in a wide arc. Kovo could not commune with other beasts, but even so, he knew the meaning of their falcon cries: This was where the burning piece of sky was to land.

It was a place Kovo knew well. A place every creature knew.

The tree.

The tree was sacred. Its roots stretched to every corner of the world. Every blade of grass, every beating heart, had sprung from it. And now the sky was plummeting toward it.

Kovo remembered wondering what would happen when the piece of sky reached the tree. A thing like this had never happened before.

The silverbacks in Kovo's tribe gathered together. One of them should go to the place where the falcons flew—to bring back news of the thing that fell. They needed a young ape who could still move quickly through the trees. Someone who could be trusted not to become lost or distracted by the creatures and sights beyond their jungle canopy. They picked Kovo.

It was a great honor. And before Kovo left, the elder ape began to sing for him, cooing into the night air. He was joined by the others, one by one, in a chorus more wonderful than anything Kovo had heard since.

Kovo's mother joined last. Her hands found his and she pressed her nose to Kovo's. To this day, he still remembered the smell of her.

Kovo left the safety of the canopy in search of the place where the sky would land. The world was a vast continent that contained jungles and dunes and mountains and snowfields, all connected together. As he traveled, he saw other beasts moving in the same direction as him: a lion from the plains, an octopus from the sulfur delta, a serpent from the desolate bogs, even a polar bear from the high glacier rim. Usually Kovo would have tried to fight with these beasts, or they would have fought with him, but it seemed they all had a similar mission.

Kovo and the other beasts finally found themselves at the top of a high mountain covered in lush vegetation and strange greenery. There were thousands of animals, all different species, all come to bear witness. The trees were low and not good for climbing, but they were heavy-laden with fruit. Kovo did not recognize the fruits growing in this place, and so he ate nothing.

At last he reached the tree. It stood within an emptied mountain—its trunk impossibly tall. The enormous, lush branches stretched out in every direction, strong and silvery. Kovo could feel the tree's life-giving roots whispering in the rich soil beneath him. He climbed atop a large, mossy boulder and watched the falling piece of sky. From here, Kovo could see the land stretching out for a thousand miles in every direction.

By now, the piece of sky burned as large and hot as a second sun. The speck had a trail of flames behind it, as though it were leaving a tear in the very atmosphere, roaring as it hurtled straight toward the tree. The roaring reverberated through the entire forest around Kovo, and many of the watching beasts fled in terror. Kovo felt that same fear, but he did not run. The fur on his arms had a static tingle of expectation. He wanted to hold his breath.

And then it landed.

Kovo shielded his eyes as the great piece of sky crashed through the branches of the tree and plunged deep into its trunk. When it finally struck the ground, the impact was like nothing Kovo had ever conceived.

In a flicker, the trees all around him bent sideways, as if they were blades of grass flattened under Kovo's foot. The sound, if it made a sound, was so great that Kovo's ears stopped working—his head filled with a devastating thrum that threatened to crack his skull in two. The ground beneath Kovo seemed to ripple and heave, throwing him backward.

And then there was the storm.

At the moment of impact, a burst of blinding light struck Kovo—searing his eyes through his eyelids. Wind and fire enveloped the sky, everything around him coming ablaze. It was like a crack of lightning had moved right through the land.

Kovo did not remember landing—for the next moment, his whole world went black.

When Kovo woke again, it was as though waking from death. Steam rose up from the scorched ground, burning the side of his face. The sky overhead was a swirling darkness that blotted out the sun. Kovo pushed himself up on his knuckles, retching some horrible black sap that seemed to have pooled beneath him, coating his fur. He could feel his bones screaming in protest as he stirred, and he wondered how many of them had been shattered.

Kovo rose and beheld the forest around him. But there was no forest. The trees were gone. The rocks were gone. Indeed, the very ground had been turned into an enormous smoking crater.

He looked to the place where the sky had landed.

The tree was still standing—ever standing—but its trunk was twisted and scarred, torn down the middle where the sky piece had struck it.

Kovo could still feel the life of the tree moving beneath the ground, but something about it had changed.

The tree wasn't the only thing that had changed. Despite his injuries, Kovo felt somehow stronger, and his mind felt more clear. He scrambled up over the steaming rubble to the crest of the crater.

Destruction. For miles in every direction. Huge black cracks had formed in the earth, and already he could see water flooding into the gaps, dividing earth, pushing the lands apart from one another. Storms were brewing, and he knew somehow that the rest of his tribe was gone. Perhaps other creatures from farther lands had survived the impact, but Kovo's jungle was no more.

The young ape flared his nostrils, squeezing his eyes tight. He wanted to beat his chest, to roar and rage. But who could hear such a cry? He was alone.

Kovo turned, hearing a wheezing *snuff* nearby. Rubble pushed apart and he saw the trunk of an enormous elephant burst from the earth, dripping with black sap. The beast had somehow survived, just like him. There were more sounds and soon other survivors emerged.

There were fifteen of them in all.

Like Kovo, the beasts looked different–stronger, larger than before. Kovo and the others slowly moved toward the tree in the center of the steaming crater. The thing that had fallen from the sky had burrowed deep into the earth, leaving a trail of foul black sap in its wake.

Some of the beasts were unable to make the descent, or too afraid, but Kovo had to see. He had been sent by his tribe, by the elder ape, by his mother, to witness the falling sky, and he would finish his task.

He approached the gash in the trunk of the tree. It looked so fragile, and he feared it might break under his touch. But when he grabbed hold of the smoldering bark, he could feel the tree shifting beneath his fingers– fighting back against its own destruction, forcing itself to grow anew.

The sky had plunged straight through it and deep into the ground. The hole was steep and treacherous, but Kovo felt strong and agile. Soon even the falcon and swan had given up the pursuit, but Kovo traveled on.

At last he found the bottom of the hole, deep within the roots of the tree. The space was a little bigger than the canopy where his tribe ate their meals.

The hole was so dark that Kovo could barely make out his own hand. But the silver light from the tree's roots was enough to see what he had come for. Lodged deep within the ground was something large and round.

It looked like a rock, only made of a substance Kovo had never seen before. Something strong enough to cut through the world itself.

Kovo drew in his breath. He could sense something moving beneath the surface. A tremor of life that pulsed like a heart. Something was inside, trying to get free. Kovo stepped back, staring at the thing below, and realization washed over him.

This was not sky.

This was not stone.

This was an egg.

HUNTER AND PREY

THE HOODED MAN MOVED LIKE A SHADOW BENEATH the moonlight. His skin was impossibly pale—purple veins could be seen tracing along his temple and neck, pulsing like little tendrils just beneath the flesh. The man's eyes looked inhuman—pupils so large there was almost no white to speak of. "And these travelers," he said, his lips stretched thin, like his patience. "Where are they now?"

"I do not know, sire!" Hazeel cried, his voice shaking. "The travelers docked for only a night to replenish supplies and get fresh water." It was hard for Hazeel to speak on account of being suspended by his ankles over the edge of the stone pier. A pulley and rope—meant for loading and unloading ships—was looped around his feet, leaving him dangling above the water. Thirty feet below, violent white breakers smashed against the rocks along the shore. He had been hanging like this for hours and the air had turned cold with the sinking sun. "P-p-please," he stammered. "I am only a humble harbormaster."

"You're more than that," the hooded man said, tugging off one of his leather gloves. Hazeel caught a glimpse of a tattoo running the back of his hand—a spirit animal under his control. "You are the last living person to see those I seek." The man flashed a poisonous smile. "Whether you *continue* to be living is entirely up to your friend up there."

Hazeel twisted his neck and stared above him—stared at the silver-furred rat who sat at the top of the pulley, chewing on the knot that kept Hazeel aloft. The rat was Hazeel's spirit animal, Poe. His only friend. Except Poe did not belong to Hazeel anymore. The hooded man had done something to the creature, infected him with some sort of wriggling black parasite that severed Hazeel's spirit animal bond . . . and now the rat was a slave to the hooded man.

Hazeel swallowed. Even though it was cold, he felt a rivulet of sweat running down his upside-down head. He watched Poe greedily gnawing at the strands of the rope, which was already groaning under Hazeel's weight. A few more strands and Hazeel would fall to his death.

"These travelers," the hooded man said, "did they have spirit animals with them? A falcon and a lion and a swan?"

"I saw no animals, sire," Hazeel said. But then he decided that his best tactic might be to tell the man what he clearly wanted to hear, so he quickly added: "But it would not surprise me! It was obvious they were hiding something. The entire crew wore red cloaks and masks that concealed their faces. And when they paid me, they used silver fronds—the currency of Zourtzi."

The hooded man fixed his dark-dark eyes on Hazeel. "And which way did they go when they left your port?"

"They went south. Straight for the Frozen Sea." Hazeel shook his head. "I warned them that only shipwreck awaited them in those frosty waters, but they would not listen."

The hooded man nodded, pleased with this information. He turned toward someone behind Hazeel—one of his own crewmen—and snapped his fingers. "Prepare the ship with fresh rations. We sail into the Frozen Sea. Tonight." The crewman, dressed in a green cloak, bowed and rushed to fulfill the orders.

Hazeel watched the crew, all of them dressed in tattered green cloaks. He felt a prickle of confusion—these were not the Greencloaks he knew. They all had pale faces and hideous, pulsing black marks on their brows—like coiled worms buried just beneath the flesh. Perhaps they were under the hooded man's control, like his own Poe. But when he looked at the hooded man, he saw that the man, too, had the mark. Was he also under the control of something even more powerful than himself?

Hazeel's body lurched and twisted as another strand of the rope broke under the rat's gnawing teeth. He closed his eyes, forcing himself not to look at the rocky shore below. "I've told you what you asked! Will you not release me?"

"You have set us in the right direction," the hooded man said. "And for that, I will spare your life." He clucked his tongue and Poe scampered immediately from the ropes and to the man's side—as if they'd been practicing that trick their whole lives. He turned and started walking toward the gangplank of his waiting ship.

Hazeel was overcome with relief . . . until he realized that the hooded man meant to leave him dangling above the water. "And what of me, sire?" he cried to the man's receding figure. "Will you not take me with you? It could be weeks before another ship comes to this remote port."

"You had better hope it's sooner," the man called over his shoulder.

"Sire!" Hazeel cried to the hooded man. "You will never find your quarry in those waters. It is a graveyard for ships. Even if you knew where you wanted to go, it would be impossible to get there without a guide. I'm sure you've heard tales of how in the Frozen Sea a compass's needle never stops turning—it's true. You will be chasing your own wake before sundown. I alone know those currents. Spare my life and take me with you. I will guide you to those you seek!"

The hooded man paused at the edge of the pier. "An interesting offer," he said. "But I already have a guide." He lifted up the edge of his tunic and touched a tattoo on his side that seemed to depict some sort of spotted cat. There was a flash of light, and then an enormous leopard appeared next to the man. The creature narrowed its violet eyes, licking its gleaming fangs.

Hazeel had little to show for education, but he knew enough to know what he was looking at. "Is that . . . Uraza?" he said, his voice a whisper. "The Great Beast."

"It is indeed." Zerif knelt down and pet the leopard, touching a spiral mark on her brow. "And she's all mine."

He peered into the face of the beast, whose nostrils were flared. Her fangs glowed white in the dim light, and she was growling. "I have no need for your services," the hooded man said. "Uraza is a huntress. She will lead us to her prey. And then her prey will die."

THE FROZEN SEA

ABEKE CROUCHED IN THE CROW'S NEST, STARING OUT over the choppy surface of the water that stretched clear to the white horizon. She clutched a small obsidian stone in her hand, which she was chiseling to a razor point to create an arrowhead. One of dozens she had stowed in the pack of her quiver. The water was bitterly cold, just like the air. But neither was half so cold as she was inside. She pulled her tattered cloak around her shoulders, but even that gave little comfort. She wore the colors of a Greencloak, but what right did she have to such a title? Greencloaks had spirit animals. And Abeke had nothing.

The ship, a creaking frigate named the *Expiator*, keeled to one side, and Abeke had to grip the ropes of the crow's nest to prevent being flung into the water a hundred feet below. Beneath her, she could hear the sounds of the crew working the lines to keep the ship upright as they charted a course ever southward. She and Rollan had been traveling for several days, moving swiftly through an uncharted sea whose only reputation was for storm and shipwreck. Even now, she could see the jagged shards of floating ice that stuck from the water's surface like fifty-foot teeth, waiting to devour them. Cold wind shivered past the top of the mast, and she wondered how many ships had found their ends in these waters. And where did these waters even lead? All they had been told was that they were being carried to a place called "the snare," but none of the crew was willing to tell her more.

Abeke was startled from her work by the sound of someone ascending the rungs. "Mind if I join you?"

She glanced over her shoulder to see Rollan hoisting himself up onto the deck of the crow's nest. His face was chapped from the cold, and she knew that he, like her, was unused to such weather. That he had come upon her so stealthily was not surprising, but it was distressing. If Uraza had still been with her, Abeke would have sensed his approach.

"Shouldn't you be babysitting our new recruits?" she said, helping him up the top rung. Rollan had been tasked with keeping tabs on two newer children who had recently summoned Great Beasts, Kirat and Tasha. The thought of Rollan playing the role of Greencloak mentor almost made her smile. Quite a change from the boy who once loudly claimed to care for no one but himself. She suspected their own mentor, the late Tarik, would have shared her amusement.

"I set Kirat to swabbing the latrine," Rollan said. "Thought it would build character." He dug into the pockets of the fur-lined coat that the Redcloaks had given him and removed a rasher of dried shark meat. "I swiped a second helping of lunch. Thought you might be getting hungry up here. . . ." But even as he said this, his eyes fell on the pile of untouched food at her feet—several days' worth of rations.

Abeke gave a tight smile. "Not a big fan of seafood, I'm afraid." The truth was, she hadn't eaten in two days. She simply didn't have an appetite. "It gives me a bad stomach."

Abeke saw worry flash across Rollan's face, which he quickly replaced with a forced grin. "Oh, well. More for me!" He chomped down on a strip of meat and settled in beside her, apparently unable to take the hint that she wanted to be alone.

The deck of the crow's nest was designed for one adult, and there was hardly enough room for the two of them. Rollan sat with his back against Abeke's, each of them staring out in a different direction.

"You haven't seen Essix up here, have you?" he said through bites of shark meat. "She's been acting strange for days now, swooping around in big uneven loops, high then low then high again. . . . I can feel her uncertainty, as if the air were making her dizzy. If I didn't know better, I'd say she's been nipping at the Redcloaks' grog barrels."

He probably meant this as a joke, but Abeke couldn't manage even a smile. "I tried bringing her into passive state, but the moment I did that, *I* started feeling dizzy, too. Just this morning I threw up my whole breakfast on the deck. Hence the fresh appetite." He sighed, chuckling. "I swear that bird will be the end of me. My life would be ten times easier if I'd gotten a three-toed sloth . . . or maybe a nice, slow beetle. A beetle would have been grand!"

Abeke pulled her knees tight against her chest. "At least you *have* a spirit animal," she said quietly.

She felt Rollan take a deep breath behind her. For once, he seemed to be at a loss for a witty retort. "Wonder how much farther it is to this mysterious Redcloak base?" he asked more seriously. "Never imagined a place could be so crushingly cold. No life, hardly any fish even. Just huge chunks of jagged ice. This place makes Suka's ice palace look positively cozy."

Abeke nodded, smiling despite herself. What felt like a lifetime before, she and Rollan had ventured to the northernmost mountains of Eura to find the talisman of the Great Bear, Suka. But that particular talisman had been stolen by Shane, the Devourer. The very same Shane who now captained the ship they were traveling aboard. Even now, it was unclear whether they were guests or prisoners.

"Do you really think we can trust them?" Rollan said, as if reading her thoughts. "I know they saved our lives back in Nilo—more than once, even. But still. We've been deceived before."

Abeke eyed the crew moving far below, all of them wearing long red cloaks and cloth masks over their faces. Each mask was marked with the image of a different animal. The masks provided some warmth from the bitter cold, but that was not why they wore them.

These "Redcloaks" wore masks to hide their faces. Every single one of them, down to the last woman and man, had a pair of inhuman eyes peering out from the folds of her or his mask. The few who had been bold enough to take their masks off around Abeke and the others revealed patches of skin that were disfigured into a twisted hash of animal and human.

Abeke still wasn't sure what had happened to produce this strange result, but it was unnerving to say the least. Shane himself had greeted her in Nilo with the cruel yellow eyes of a reptile—the eyes of his lost spirit animal.

Perhaps that was no less than he deserved. The boy's crocodile tears had once convinced her to lead him right into Greenhaven, where he promptly betrayed her. That Shane now wore the symbol of his deception seemed only fitting.

But thinking of Shane and his crocodile only made her think of Uraza. Abeke closed her eyes, remembering the moment when Zerif's parasite infected her beloved spirit animal. How Uraza's violet eyes had suddenly clouded over. And worse than that, how a part of Abeke's own heart and soul had just as suddenly *vanished*.

Once in control of Uraza, Zerif had ordered the leopard to kill Abeke . . . and Uraza had *listened*. Without a moment's hesitation, Uraza had pounced at her, claws out. Had it not been for Cabaro intercepting the attack, Abeke would be dead. But then, how much worse could death really be from what she was already feeling?

All that would have been difficult enough for Abeke to process, but the recent discovery that the leader of the Redcloaks was none other than Shane—the Devourer who had once set out to destroy them all—was more than she could handle. She had trusted Shane once before and paid a dear price for it. And yet here she was, sailing to a secret location on a ship under his command.

But what choice did they have? With Zerif's army of infected Greencloaks hunting down the other Great Beasts, they had nowhere else to turn.

"I don't know if we can trust him," Abeke said at last. "But when I look at him now . . . some part of me thinks he really has changed."

"Oh, he's changed all right—into a lizard-eyed freak. If anything, he looks more like the Devourer than ever before. Not exactly reassuring."

"Still," Abeke said. "If he wanted us dead, he could have just let Zerif do the job. He needs us for something. It's just a question of what." She shivered, pulling her cloak tighter. "Wherever he's taking us, let's hope we get there before we freeze to death."

Their conversation was interrupted by a faint cry of a bird. "It's Essix!" Rollan said, climbing to his feet. "She sees something." The cry had come from far ahead, somewhere deep in the clouds. Abeke watched as Rollan closed his eyes and put a hand to his temple—trying to *see* through his spirit animal's eyes. Abeke had seen him do this many times before, but only now did it fill her with a pang of jealousy. A moment later he stepped back, blinking. He had the slack-jawed look of someone who had just beheld a wonder beyond his own imagining.

"What is it?" Abeke said, standing. "Did you see the Place of Desolation?"

"One thing's for sure," he said, shaking his head in disbelief. "We're not going to freeze to death."

THE MOLTEN RUINS

Growing up in Amaya as he had, Rollan had certainly heard stories about volcanoes—tales of long-dead kingdoms now buried under blankets of petrified ash. But none of those stories had captured just how awesome it was to behold an *actual* live volcano. Rollan had seen it first through Essix's eyes, and then only for a brief moment—a glowing red cauldron spewing miles of steam into the cold air. His falcon had returned to him shortly after, and she seemed grateful for the chance to rest herself on the edge of the mast.

It was nearly an hour before the *Expiator* came within view of the steaming black mountain that towered over the horizon. Having only seen it from Essix's eyes overhead, Rollan was unprepared for its size. The volcano was *massive*—large enough to hold half of his home city of Concorba inside of it.

"I'll say one thing for our friend Shane," he muttered to Abeke. "He knows how to make an impression."

"Land ho!" a female Redcloak with a bird mask called,

ringing a bell on the ship's fore. "All hands to the main deck!"

Rollan and Abeke went belowdecks to find Kirat and Tasha and gather what few belongings they had managed to bring with them when they fled Zerif's army back in Nilo. They came upon Tasha practicing the defensive forms that Rollan had taught her, a large staff gripped tightly in her hands. In the past few weeks she had shown herself to be a dedicated student . . . though it had quickly become apparent that stationary fighting positions were best suited for the girl. Tasha couldn't seem to walk ten steps without tripping over her own feet.

Kirat, meanwhile, was caught in yet another battle of wills with his Great Beast. Proud, fierce Cabaro was apparently as prone to seasickness as Uraza had been, and had hidden himself under Kirat's bunk, refusing to leave even for meals.

"I'm trying to *help you*, you overgrown house cat!" Kirat said, hands in the air. "If you go passive, I can escort you down to land myself. Everybody wins!"

In reply, the lion bared his white teeth and growled.

Kirat showed his own teeth, which were chattering in the cold. "When you die down there, I think I'll have you turned into a nice fur coat. At least then you'll be of some use to me."

Rollan put a hand on Kirat's shoulder. "Leave him. He'll come out when he's ready. I know from experience there's no use commanding a stubborn spirit animal. They're Great Beasts. Not servants."

As he said this, he couldn't help but glance at Essix, who had perched herself on his right arm, refusing to move from that spot. The gyrfalcon gripped him so tightly that he could feel it through his thick leather gauntlet. Rollan suspected that whatever strange disruption the falcon had felt in the air had made her wary of flying. He reached up and scratched her under the beak, and surprisingly she let him. Whatever it was about this place that made her so uncomfortable, he hoped it faded soon. He didn't want to find himself in a fight without Essix at his side.

Their packs gathered, Rollan and the others were summoned by a Redcloak called Stead who wore the mask of a ram.

"King has gone ahead. You four are to follow me," the boy said, in the tone of one who was used to having his orders obeyed. "Watch your step on the gangplank. If you fall into the water, you'll be frozen before we can fish you out."

The base of the volcano was encased in the thick shell of an enormous icy glacier. Rivulets of steaming red lava snaked through the ice, filling the air with a damp, sulfurous odor. The *Expiator* had been docked at a pier that looked to have been chiseled out of the side of the glacier. Small huts and glistening bridges were similarly cut from the ice. Rollan and the others shuffled down the gangplank and onto the glacier's surface. Unlike the snow up north, the ground here was hard and ungiving—the sort that would hurt to fall on.

"Careful," Rollan said as Tasha rushed down the platform right behind him. He heard a cry as the girl slipped on her *very first* step on the ice and landed hard on her rump—her pack spilling out behind her. "Maybe we can fashion you a sled," Rollan said, reaching down to help her to her feet. "Ninani can pull it."

Tasha ignored his extended hand. She swung her foot around, sweeping Rollan's leg from behind and sending him crashing onto the ice beside her. He felt his face grow hot as every Redcloak watching burst into laughter. "On the bright side," he said, wincing as he pulled himself back up, "at least I know you've been practicing."

Stead led them up some narrow steps that curved around the edge of the volcano, providing them an overhead view of the camp. Glancing below, Rollan saw that everyone was wearing red cloaks—except for a small pack of kids just a bit younger than him. There were maybe a half dozen of them, all wearing sealskin coats.

"What's the story with them?" Rollan said, nodding at the group. "You ran out of red fabric?"

"I'm surprised you haven't guessed," Stead said, his voice heavy. "Those are the other victims of Zerif's parasites. Kids like you, who summoned Great Beasts as spirit animals."

Squinting down, Rollan realized that he recognized the face of Anda among the other kids—the Amayan boy who had summoned Tellun. But how had he ended up here? The last time Rollan and Abeke had seen Anda was in Greenhaven. Olvan had been preparing to send him back home to Amaya.

"Zerif tracked them all down and stole their spirit animals," Stead said, "sometimes destroying their homes and families in the process. They're here to take back what was stolen from them." It was all Rollan could do not to sneak a glance at Abeke, who undoubtedly recognized her own pain in their hollow faces.

The children were all working diligently, helping to dig trenches in the ice, cooking food, mending boots. The idea that these Redcloaks had managed to gather the other Great Beast summoners—while he and Abeke had failed—irked Rollan. "Must be nice to have your own personal army of servants," he muttered.

Stead turned and regarded Rollan through his strange white mask. "They aren't our servants," he said finally. "They're here because King rescued them. He wants to help." Then he turned and began scaling the path again.

"What we really need is an army of fighters," Stead continued as he walked. "But it's too late to train these children. Especially without their spirit animals." He cocked his head to one side, studying Rollan. "Or maybe you could help with that? I hear you have a gift for mentoring young warriors."

Rollan couldn't tell if he was being mocked or not, but the proposition horrified him. "Not me," he said, nodding to Kirat and Tasha. "I've paid my dues with these two, and that was plenty. Trying to teach Kirat anything is like trying to get Cabaro into passive state. Impossible."

Kirat scowled. "Maybe if you actually knew what you were doing, I would listen."

Rollan looked at the boy, who was the very picture of smugness. That this boy was the nephew of Rollan's old mentor, Tarik, was almost impossible to believe. He thought of the amulet resting at the bottom of his pack. The amulet that Kirat's mother had given him. It was Rollan's job to hold on to it until Kirat had matured enough to follow in his uncle's footsteps. At the rate things were presently going, Rollan would die of old age before that happened.

"Think you can do better?" Rollan said, nodding to the children working below. "Be my guest."

He had meant it as a joke, but Kirat seemed to consider the idea. The boy folded his arms. "Maybe I will."

"Later," Stead said, interrupting the contest of wills. "Right now we should eat, before King comes. He's going to want to talk to you."

"King . . . ?" Abeke said. "That's what you call Shane?"

Stead nodded. "He tells us not to, but . . . old habits die hard."

Rollan looked at Abeke, trying to read her face. The Shane they knew would probably have forced people to call him king on punishment of death. It was hard to imagine him as anything but a ruthless leader. "Stay close," he whispered as they followed Stead up the snowy path. "And keep your bow handy."

Rollan and the others soon found themselves sitting in an alcove carved into the side of the mountain. A small group of Redcloaks joined them there, but stood aloof several feet away. It was as if they were afraid of Rollan and Abeke. Afraid . . . or ashamed.

Stead removed his mask to reveal a pair of horizontal pupils in his eyes—just like a ram.

The other Redcloaks appeared to be from all different parts of the world. As they slowly removed their masks, Rollan saw a girl with the flitting black eyes of a bird, a man with pinhole pupils like a lizard, and another with sad, doglike eyes and a rash of long fur that crept up his neck. It was all Rollan could do not to stare.

Though the air outside was frigid, the temperature in the alcove was comfortable. A vein of red lava flowed through a man-made channel that ran around the perimeter, warming the ground just enough so Rollan could breathe without his teeth chattering. The Redcloaks outside were busy tending to an enormous cauldron of stew that was hanging over a pool of bubbling lava.

Stead was watching them, his strange eyes moving between the figures. Many of their masks were off now. It seemed they were preparing to eat. "This is Shadow," Stead said, gesturing to a woman with catlike eyes.

"And these"—he nodded toward two boys who had kept their masks on—some kind of wildcat and a bird with a long straight beak—"are Worthy and Jolt. Though you may already know them by different names."

The boys slowly removed their masks, and Rollan's mouth fell open. Beside him, Abeke sucked in a hiss of air. Standing before them were none other than Devin Trunswick and Karmo—two of the young Conquerors they'd beaten back in Eura while searching for Rumfuss's talisman.

In the handful of brief and unpleasant encounters he'd had with Devin, Rollan had never once seen the boy without a sneer. Now the Euran noble's catlike eyes seemed weighted to the ground—like he was ashamed to be seen.

Karmo's own wide brown eyes were on Abeke, who glared right back at him.

There was a great deal of glaring back and forth, in fact. Stead coughed uncomfortably.

It was Devin who broke the silence. "So . . ." he said, his eyes finally rising. "How's Conor?"

Rollan barked out a hard laugh and shook his head. "If this is your idea of a joke," he said, "I'm not looking forward to the punch line."

"It's no joke," Stead said, sighing. "King suspected you'd be mistrustful. I don't blame you. But know this—Worthy and Jolt, like all of us, are here to atone for their crimes."

Rollan decided to take the boy at his word . . . at least for now. "So you all get to pick secret names?" he said. "Can I request that people start calling me Handsome?"

"Most names are based on our spirit animals," said another Redcloak woman with black, hungry eyes that reminded him of a bat. "So maybe we should call you Featherbrain?"

The others all laughed at this jibe, and even Abeke smirked. Rollan was annoyed at being the object of ridicule, but also surprised. Up to this point the Redcloaks had been completely humorless. But seeing them crouched around the stewpot, he wondered if the things they'd endured had built a bond between them . . . just like the bond he felt with Abeke, Conor, and Meilin.

Perhaps Stead was being more forthright than Rollan gave him credit for. This *wasn't* an army. These were friends.

Rollan took a seat with Abeke, Kirat, and Tasha. Karmo—*Jolt*—served them steaming bowls of what smelled like fish stew.

"Ugh," Kirat said, wrinkling his nose. "More fish."

"At least it's hot," Rollan said, spooning sips into his mouth. "If experience has taught me one thing, it's that you never turn down a hot meal. You never know if it will be your last." He quickly finished his bowl and passed it back for another. He couldn't help but notice that Abeke accepted a bowl, too, but only held it in her hands to warm herself.

"Guess I'm not very hungry," she said with a weak smile when she noticed Rollan watching her. "Maybe Essix wants it?"

She set the stew on the ground. Rollan stared at Abeke's face, at her blank expression, almost devoid of life or energy. Was that what it meant to lose a spirit animal? The thought made him shudder. Strained though his relationship with Essix could be at times, he couldn't fathom the pain of not having her with him.

Essix hopped down to the offered bowl, pecking at the contents as best as she could. Rollan reached down and pet her cowl, glad for the reassuring touch of her presence.

There was a sound of footsteps echoing off hard stone. All at once, the relaxed manner of the Redcloaks changed as they put down their bowls and sprang to attention.

"Now that you've all eaten," said a voice from behind them, "it's time we get down to business."

Rollan looked up to see Shane standing in the mouth of a tunnel, his figure lit orange against the magma glow. He had taken his mask off, and Rollan was again struck by his changed appearance—his yellow crocodile eyes and the glimpse of scaly green flesh creeping up his neck.

Shane had once been a strong, handsome ruler—heir to the throne of Stetriol. Now he looked like a monster.

The boy stepped into the middle of the room with the bearing of a king. Rollan had to begrudgingly admit that the name fit. "I'm sure you're all curious why I've brought you here," Shane began.

"I assumed we would go sledding," Rollan said. "Maybe have a nice snowball fight."

Shane ignored him and took a seat on a rock, facing the group. "We Redcloaks . . ." He paused and shook his head, as if unable or unwilling to say what needed to be said. "I'm sure you've recognized some former Conquerors among our people. Worthy and Jolt you've even fought personally."

"And suddenly you're acting like our best friends," Rollan said. "It's downright creepy . . . and don't even get me started on your weird faces. I get why you guys use masks."

"Watch it!" Stead said, leaping to his feet, one hand on his sword.

"*Stead*," Shane said in a commanding voice. The young man stopped, still glaring at Rollan, his jaw clenched. Finally he sat back down. Shane turned back to them. "Forgive our hot tempers. It's a sensitive subject for some of us."

"What happened to you all?" Abeke said, her voice hoarse. "I think you owe us that much, at least."

Shane watched her for a long moment, then nodded. "It's hard not to think of it as a punishment. Every one of us drank Gerathon's Bile. When the Bile's power faded, most Conquerors simply lost their spirit animals. Freed from our control, the beasts either attacked their former masters or fled. For a small number, however, there was no escape. One day I awoke to find I couldn't summon Grahv from his passive form. The tattoo on my chest began to itch and fade, and in its place I found . . ."

Shane lifted his shirt, revealing a wide swathe of green, scaly skin where Rollan had once seen a crocodile's jaw curving around his neck.

The former king of Stetriol let out a husky sigh. "It's the same for all the others. Somehow, our spirit animals have become a part of us. Any gifts they gave us in their active states—strength, speed, uncanny powers—have returned, but at the cost of our humanity. We are all changing. Into what, I can't say."

"How awful," Tasha said. Her clear blue eyes were wide with pity.

"I suppose it is," Shane said. "But we have so much to atone for. Me most of all." Even behind Shane's eerie stare, Rollan thought he could detect genuine pain in his face. "What we did in the war, what I did to all of you—" He looked up for a moment, his yellow gaze set on Abeke. "There's nothing I can do to fix it . . . no matter how I wish I could." He shook his head, blinking at the ground.

"Is that it?" Rollan said. "You dragged us here so you could apologize? You could have written a letter and saved us all a lot of time."

"This is not just about me, or what I've done." Shane took a deep breath. "I brought you here because I need your help. Erdas needs your help." He turned his yellow gaze on Rollan. "There's someone you need to meet— someone who needs to talk to you."

Rollan rolled his eyes. He was getting tired of Shane's dramatics. "And where is this mysterious someone?"

A creaking voice whispered beneath his feet. "She's right here, birdyboy."

The voice was so close to Rollan that he immediately shouted out in surprise and leaped clear off his seat, fumbling for his dagger. The bowl of stew that he'd been holding flew up into the air and landed with a loud *slosh!* right on his head.

Rollan spun around, staring at the person who had spoken to him. It was an old woman with cracked, leathery skin, laughing with a huge toothless smile. She was lying on the ground at his feet, arms at her side. Her white hair was tangled and greasy, hanging limp from her thin face. And her eyes . . . were *gone*. Where two eyes should have been there were only soft dents in the flesh—as if someone had sculpted her from clay and forgotten that one feature.

Rollan wiped fish stew from his face, still breathing heavily. For the third time in less than an hour, he was surrounded by laughing Redcloaks. He glanced down at Essix, who seemed similarly amused. "Very funny," he muttered, flinging boiled fish guts from his cloak.

"Sorry to have startled you, birdyboy," the old woman said, then sniffed the air. "Or is it fishyboy? I can't tell for sure." She reached a gnarled finger toward him and scooped a glop of fish stew from his shin. Then she put it into her mouth, tasting. Apparently the crone approved of the taste, because the next moment she reached out again for more.

"Get off me!" Rollan cried, shoving her back. He turned toward Shane, blade raised. "Who is this crazy old bat?"

The old woman moved closer, wriggling across the ground. "I am no bat, birdyboy. Yumaris is an *earth-worm*!" She scrunched up her face. "So tiny I can wriggle through the cracks of the world. So quiet I can hear the whisperings of *tomorrow* . . . or is it yesterday?" She shook her head, as though confused about the difference between the two.

"Her name is Yumaris," said a quiet voice. Rollan was surprised to see that it was Abeke who had spoken. Her voice sounded different, tense. "She was one of the Conquerors with Gar," Abeke went on. "I saw her when Zerif brought me to Gar the first time, and then again when Meilin and I were taken prisoner. I think she was a seer of some kind."

The old woman clapped her hands. "Not just *was*, hollow-girl! For all my blindness, Yumaris remains a seer still. And what I see now . . ." She shook her head, her strands of limp hair swaying back and forth. "What I see now . . ." Apparently whatever the old woman "saw" was too much to speak of, and she started muttering, twisting at the ends of her hair. The next moment she was talking to the tips of her fingers, like each of them was a little pet.

"Great," Rollan said, sitting back down. "You dragged us halfway around the world to meet a crazy person."

"Yumaris *is* crazy," Shane agreed. "And dangerous." It was clear from the tone of his voice that he might have resented the woman's help. Rollan wondered what else had transpired between the two of them. "But she's also useful. In these times, we can't afford the luxury of picking our allies."

"Tell me about it," Rollan said, snorting.

"Her visions have kept us alive these last months," Shane continued. "And they led us to these ruins, where even Zerif couldn't find us. She wasn't always quite this . . . eccentric. Her spirit animal was an earthworm that gave her glimpses of the future. When she inherited these powers in full . . . Well, she's a bit confused now."

"She thinks she's an earthworm," Stead said flatly.

Rollan watched Yumaris, who was currently trying to claw her way into the rocky wall with her bare hands. It looked painful. She gave up with her hands and started chewing the rock. "So why bring us to her?" Rollan said.

Shane met his eyes, his face deadly serious. "Because she's the only thing standing between us and the destruction of the world."

THE SNARE

THEIR MEALS FINISHED, SHANE ROSE AND APPROACHED a narrow tunnel. "Stead, please take Tasha and Kirat to the others, and help them set up camp."

"We're not here to do servants' work," Kirat said, standing. "We're coming with you." Cabaro was similarly inclined and growled in agreement.

"You seem to think you have some authority in this place, *little lord*," Shane said, leaning against the rock wall. Rollan smiled to himself, thinking that Shane might dislike Kirat as much as he did. "Everyone does their part here. The truth is we only brought you along to keep Cabaro away from Zerif. I'm just as happy to throw you in a cell, if you'd prefer. What I have to say is for Greencloaks alone."

Out of the corner of his eye, Rollan saw Abeke lower her head. "Then maybe I should join the others," she said.

"Stop that!" Rollan swatted her arm. "You're still a Greencloak—spirit animal or not. And there's no way I'm going to follow Mistress Wormbrain and King

Lizardface into a steaming volcano without some backup." He made a stern face to show her that he was only half kidding. That he really did need her.

Abeke rolled her eyes, but Rollan could tell she was doing it to conceal a smile. He couldn't possibly imagine what it would be like to lose a spirit animal, but he knew that without Uraza, Abeke needed a friend now more than ever.

"King," Stead said, approaching Shane, "there was some talk of Kirat training the other Great Beast summoners in combat. Perhaps he can do that instead of chores?"

Shane considered it. "It couldn't hurt. Very well." He signaled for Stead to lead Kirat and Tasha to the outer camp.

Rollan and Abeke followed Shane and Yumaris down a steep tunnel staircase that seemed to go straight into the base of the volcano. Steaming pools of lava filled the cold air with an eerie red glow. "Are you sure it's safe to chisel away the walls of a volcano?" Rollan said, hopping over a hissing puddle of lava. "What if you, um, spring a leak?"

"That's not likely," Shane said. "These tunnels were here long before we arrived. The ruins themselves are carved from some kind of rock that doesn't melt— something mined deep within the ground."

He led them past a small balcony that overlooked the inside of the volcano. Where Rollan had expected a molten lake, he instead found an enormous round stone door made of overlapping blades that intersected in the middle—like the folds of an iris.

"The main volcano cauldron has been stopped up for centuries," Shane explained. "The lava you're seeing here is all flowing from cracks in and around the surface. So long as you watch your step, you should be fine. Plus it helps light the way."

As they circled around the floor of the ruins, Rollan noticed a towering shard of ice in the center of the cavern—a frost-covered stalagmite that was nearly as tall as the mountain. "What's with the giant icicle?" he said.

Shane shrugged, peering up at the tower. "We're not sure. There's some sort of structure underneath, but cold air from the mouth of the volcano has encased whatever it is in a sheet of ice too thick to penetrate. The tower is clearly connected to the ruins, but until we learn more, we've decided to leave it alone."

The path inside the mountain was not a straight line; rather it crisscrossed and branched a dozen times over to create an enormous maze. They continued turning one way, then the next, descending deeper underground.

"Stay with the group and keep your eyes open," Shane said. "If you get lost in here, it could be days before we find you again. . . . That is, if you manage not to fall down a lava flue first."

Despite his warning, the party was not being led by Shane. Yumaris guided the group, running her hands along the walls, sniffing the air, and getting into arguments with the stones.

Rollan watched her scramble down to her knees and rub her hair into the ground. "You sure the old lady's fit to guide us?" he said.

"If Shane trusts Yumaris, then so should we," Abeke

said firmly. "He's got more reason to hate her than most. She helped kill his sister."

Rollan looked up at Shane, whose face was half covered in shadow. "The past is the past," the boy said curtly. "Like the rest of us, Yumaris is trying to make up for old sins."

Rollan eyed the old woman, presently sniffing some dirt she found on the tunnel ground. "Yeah, she seems really torn up about it."

Yumaris popped the dirt into her mouth, made a face, and spit it out. "I can feel things," she whispered. "Vibrations echoing deep underground. Footsteps long passed and footsteps not yet come."

"That's how you and your Redcloaks were able to track us," Abeke said to Shane. "Yumaris could sense where we were moving."

"Exactly," Shane said. "But it was all we could do to keep up with Zerif. He's clearly got his own way of tracking the Great Beasts, and it won't be long before he finds us here." He put his hand along the rock wall. "Luckily these ruins aren't without natural defenses. When he gets here, we'll be ready."

"What exactly is this place?" Rollan said. He had by now noticed that the walls were covered in all manner of carvings. "Some kind of lost temple?"

"Not exactly a temple," Shane said. "The ruins are an ancient trap. The work of Hellan priests that lived here centuries ago."

"The *Hellans*?" said Rollan. "Someone needs to brush up on his geography." Rollan had never had any formal schooling, but even he knew about the ancient Hellans.

They were a people who lived in the garden paradise of Athenos a thousand years ago. "Hellans worshipped the sun and walked around barefoot. Why would they travel all the way to this frigid rock? That's completely insane." He glanced nervously at Yumaris. "No offense."

"Yes, offense!" Yumaris exclaimed merrily.

"That's true about Athenos," Shane said, "But these carvings tell a different story. The Hellans were more far-traveled than we realized. One group of Hellan priests exiled themselves here, to the bottommost pole of the world."

"Not a pole! A *hole*!" Yumaris chimed in. "It's the *gullet* of Erdas, what runs from tail to tip."

Rollan was a bit confused by all this, but Abeke seemed to follow. "So this volcano is at the world's axis," she said. "Well, that would explain what's gotten into Essix." She pointed to the falcon, who still sat perched on Rollan's arm. "She can barely keep upright in this place."

Rollan scrunched up his face. "What would that have to do with how she flies?"

Abeke explained, "In Nilo, every spring would bring huge flocks of homing cranes, traveling thousands of miles to a specific lake . . . almost as if they had a map and compass. Our village Greencloak once told me that the birds followed magnetic currents that moved with the tides—that's how they knew how to find their way home each year. If we're at the bottom of the world, then those invisible currents are stronger than anything Essix has ever felt . . . strong enough to completely scramble her sense of direction."

"It's true," Shane said. "A few of our Redcloaks were

bonded with birds. They find themselves constantly disoriented."

Rollan wasn't so sure. The idea that the Great Beast Essix could be bested by some "invisible currents" was alarming to say the least. And what would happen if they faced Zerif's army in this place? Rollan would be as alone as Abeke. "So why did the Hellans build all this?" he said, returning to the subject at hand. "And why risk your own life just to show it to us?"

"These ruins are more than just some remote outpost. This whole place is an enormous snare." Shane fixed his yellow eyes on Rollan. "They built it to stop something called . . . the Wyrm."

Just hearing this word made Yumaris shriek in terror. "The Wyrm! The Wyrm!" she cried. "I can hear it, uncoiling in its foul egg . . . hatching deep below! We must hide! Hide!" And the next thing Rollan knew, she had scattered off down some dark tunnel, abandoning the rest of the group.

Shane shook his head, like he had seen this before. "She can really run when she puts her mind to it. I should know better than to mention the Wyrm in her presence. She'll be useless for the rest of the day."

"How *ever* will we survive?" Rollan said with mock despair.

"I've heard of the Wyrm before," Abeke said. "Zerif mentioned it when we fought in Amaya. He said it was awakening, and that *he* was awakening with it."

"If Zerif likes it, then I hate it," Rollan said. "So what exactly is this Wyrm thing? Some kind of fancy new spirit animal?"

"I don't think it's new," Shane said, continuing

down the path. "I think it's older than the Great Beasts. And if I'm reading these carvings correctly, it's the source of the parasites—everyone who is infected is somehow drawn to the Wyrm, forced to do its bidding."

Rollan knew this wasn't quite true. "Hate to contradict you, boss, but we've seen the effects of the parasites firsthand. Everyone infected is under Zerif's control, not some Wyrm. Once they're infected, beasts and humans alike do exactly what he commands." He tried not to look at Abeke when he said this—recalling how Uraza had tried to attack her in Nilo.

"That may be true," Shane said. "But what if *something else* is controlling Zerif? What if he, too, is being used by the Wyrm?"

"Zerif commands an army of humans and spirit animals," Abeke said. "Could this Wyrm possibly be so powerful?"

"I don't know," Shane said, shrugging. "Gerathon could exert control over those of us who drank the Bile, but not on this level. All I know is what these carvings tell us. They say that the Wyrm's egg fell from the stars and landed in a place called Sadre, deep under the earth. It's been living dormant underground for centuries. Until now. The Wyrm is waking, and when it hatches, it will devour everything in its path."

Rollan swallowed. "Conor and Meilin are underground. They were trapped after falling into some hidden doorway. You're saying they're down there with that thing?"

"Possibly," Shane said. "And my source tells me they had another with them, a boy named Takoda, who summoned his own Great Beast."

All of this was true, but Rollan was surprised that Shane knew it. "Just how many spies do you have?" he said.

Shane shrugged. "Only one—but he's *very* good at his job. I'm taking you to meet him now."

Shane pointed to the wall beside him, which was etched with drawings of ancient figures digging holes at different points on the globe, meeting in the middle. "According to these carvings, the volcano was drained to make room for some kind of snare. Beneath those doors in the floor of the chamber is a tunnel that goes clear down through the center of Erdas. And somewhere in the middle is a thing called the Chamber of Tides. It's a construction powerful enough to stop the Wyrm."

"So if the Hellans completed the trap," Rollan said, "then why haven't they used it yet? Why is the Wyrm still alive?"

"It's not so easy," Shane said, and he led them down the corridor. "This trap can't be sprung until *after* the Wyrm hatches. And it's unclear how we're supposed to open the doors and activate the trap—they wanted to keep that a secret. If we're reading the carvings correctly, there's only one living soul who knows how to activate the snare. The same one who helped build this place. Though getting his help might be difficult."

"I'd imagine so!" Rollan quipped. "This place is thousands of years old. Whoever built it is probably a *bit* indisposed at the moment. Dead like the rest of the Hellans."

"Unless . . ." Abeke said. "They weren't *human* hands." She turned to Shane. "The one you're speaking of wasn't a Hellan, was he? You're talking about a Great Beast?"

"A Great Beast built this place?" Rollan said. "Which one?"

"An old friend of ours," Shane said as he rounded a corner. He pointed into the shadows toward a face carved into the stone. Rollan peered through the lava-lit corridor and stared at the carving. It was a large face, with a heavy brow, dark eyes, and sharp fangs. It was a face of pure evil.

"Kovo?" Rollan said. "You've got to be kidding."

NIRI

ABEKE GLANCED AT ROLLAN, WHOSE FACE WAS TWISTED with confused disbelief, and she thought she knew how he felt. They had just been told by Shane that Kovo—*the* Kovo—was the secret mastermind of this centuries-old plan to stop the Wyrm.

"Kovo . . . ?" she said, unable to look away from the hideous carving before her. "But he's . . . he's . . ." She shook her head, somehow unable to form a complete thought.

"He's pure evil!" Rollan burst out.

"You don't have to tell me that," Shane said. "I was as shocked as anyone."

Abeke nodded, swallowing. Shocked didn't begin to describe what she was feeling. Her hands were clammy and she could feel her heart racing in her chest. Even after all that had passed between her and Shane, so many betrayals, she still somehow believed he was trying to help. But one look at this carving and she knew the truth: Shane would never change.

"You're working for Kovo," she said, inching away from Shane, who was watching her intently. "How could I have been so stupid to trust you?"

"I'm not *working for* Kovo," Shane said to her, his voice pleading. "All I know is what the carvings have told us—that Kovo knows the secret of this place. Whether we like it or not, he is the key to destroying the Wyrm."

"You ever think that he's just trying to eliminate the competition?" Rollan said. "Kovo is evil, end of story. If he made this snare, then it can only be for his own selfish gain. We'd be fools to trust him." He shot a look at Shane. "Or you, for that matter."

"Don't forget that I saved your life," Shane said, stepping toward him. "More than once."

"Stop fighting," Abeke said. She pushed both boys apart. "Whatever we're feeling doesn't matter. Zerif's army is out there, and he's collecting Great Beasts—three of which are currently residing on this island. If we want to have a chance of stopping him *or* the Wyrm, we need to act quickly before he finds us." It wasn't exactly what she felt, but the force of her words seemed to make an impact on the boys.

"Four," Shane said quietly.

"What?" Rollan snapped.

"There are *four* Great Beasts on the island." He turned toward a narrow corridor leading away from the middle of the volcano. "Follow me."

Abeke and Rollan trailed Shane through several corners, the tunnel growing colder and colder until they reached a large chamber carved out of rock deep underground. They were far below sea level, and the tunnel *should* have been flooded. Abeke reasoned that the dip had actually trapped the air inside.

A small pool of warm water bubbled up in the middle of the floor, creating a steaming hot spring that made the air damp and salty.

Sitting at the edge of the water was a small girl with strange, almost bluish skin. She was dressed in draped cloth. Her bare legs rested in the pool, and she was weaving a blanket from strands of long seaweed.

Shane approached the girl. "Niri, say hello to our friends."

The girl put down her work and turned her head toward them. "We've been waiting for you." She said this warmly but made no effort to stand and greet them properly.

Abeke stepped closer and saw that Niri's skin was painted blue with swirling tattoos that covered her whole body. "You're from the Hundred Isles," she said. She offered a kind smile, knowing something of those tropical climes. "You must hate the snow almost as much as I do."

"Niri was there when Zerif and his army burned her entire village to the ground," Shane said darkly. "She's probably beyond hating things like weather."

"Forgive me for not standing to greet you," the girl said. "I find myself unequal to the task." She lifted the corner of her seaweed blanket to reveal that her legs were both thin and misshapen.

"Your legs don't work," Abeke said, trying not to sound horrified. "Did Zerif do that?"

"I was born unable to walk or even swim," Niri said simply. "In the Hundred Isles, our lives are lived in the sea. Not being able to swim made me an outcast. Not even the healers would agree to see me. They believed my family had violated *tapu*. My father and mother cared for me in isolation, far from shore, shunned by the rest of our tribe."

"In the end that's what saved her," Shane said. "When Zerif's army landed, all her kinsmen rushed to fight him, but she was left behind in the jungle. He burned the village down looking for Niri, but she was smart enough to keep herself hidden until the Redcloaks could rescue her."

"Why did Zerif want you?" Rollan said.

"He didn't want me," Niri said. "He wanted *him*." The girl pointed to the ceiling of the cave. There was a place where the rock had been replaced with a sheet of solid ice that shone blue light on them—sealing them off from the ocean water. The ice was cloudy, but on the other side Abeke could just make out the shadow of a large creature floating back and forth in the water. A creature with eight legs.

"Mulop!" Abeke said.

Indeed it was Mulop, and upon hearing his name spoken, the octopus swung his many arms in greeting. The Great Octopus looked smaller than when Abeke had last seen him in the grotto beyond Dagger Point, but he was still enormous. The shadow darted from view and a moment later there was a splashing at Abeke's feet as a large tentacle rose up from the pool of water and nuzzled itself against Niri's hand. Mulop's skin had an iridescent glow, like the inside of an oyster shell—a hundred colors reflecting in the cavern all around.

"Tell you honestly," Rollan said. "I'm relieved to see it's Mulop you've got down here. I was afraid we were going to be shaking hands with Gerathon!"

"Mulop saved my life in more ways than I can count," Niri said. "When Zerif attacked my village, Mulop was able to cloud the minds of his army and keep me hidden. And even before that, he changed my life. Mulop's thoughts stretch to every corner of Erdas, and he shares a connection with every living thing. Through our bond, I've felt my own senses expand, letting me experience parts of Erdas I would never have imagined. That's how I was able to sense the Redcloaks coming to my aid."

Abeke looked at the girl, her bony legs thin beneath the blanket. She wondered what it would have been like to grow up not knowing the joy of running or swimming or climbing a tree. The appearance of Mulop must have been a revelation—it was a chance at a new life.

But thinking of someone else's spirit animal only made her miss her own. She tried to picture Uraza somewhere far from here. Even knowing that the leopard was under Zerif's control, she still wished she could see her spirit animal once more.

"What do you mean by *sense*?" Rollan said, interrupting Abeke's thoughts. "Mulop gives you the power to feel the minds of others?"

Niri nodded. "He can also cloud our own minds, making *us* harder to sense—which is what he's doing right now."

"That's the reason we've been able to stay hidden from Zerif's army for so long," Shane said. "So long as

Mulop is on our side, Zerif will never be able to track us here. But the time for hiding is over. Now we need Mulop to help us find Kovo."

"Wait," Abeke said. "Kovo is underground with Meilin and Conor. Why not have him talk to Briggan?" Her mind flashed to Conor's face, sick with worry over his own infection. She hoped he was all right.

Rollan swallowed beside her. "Or maybe, um, Jhi?" Abeke glanced at the boy whose cheeks seemed to have reddened at the mention of Meilin's spirit animal. "Just a thought."

Shane shook his head. "I'm afraid we can't. Since he was reborn, Mulop's powers are considerably diminished. He'll only be able to maintain a connection for a very short time. And in order to talk to Kovo, Mulop will need to stop hiding our locations. We'll be exposed. Once that happens, Zerif will come for us. Hopefully we'll have enough time to learn how to trigger the snare."

"What if Kovo doesn't want to help?" Abeke said.

Shane met her eyes. "Then we're all as good as dead."

THE PRISONER

MEILIN DIPPED A MOSS SPONGE INTO A STONE BASIN filled with stagnant water. She wrung it out and dabbed it across Conor's burning forehead, across the dark spiral that spread along his skin like a cancer. His clothes were soaked in cold sweat, and he was shivering. "This will help the fever," she said, hoping it was true.

The boy lolled his head in her direction, swallowing with cracked lips. There were dark wells below his eyes. Conor hadn't taken food in days. "Meilin," he said, his voice faint and pleading. "Let . . . me . . . go."

"You know I can't," Meilin said. She looked down at the ropes bound around his wrists and ankles. Conor had cut deep wounds into his flesh trying to pull himself free. The wounds would become infected soon if they didn't find some way to clean them. But she knew that releasing him would be his death. Ever since setting foot in this cursed city, Conor had become overwhelmed by a desire to reach the Wyrm. He would have blindly scaled the spiraling bell tower in the middle of the city, which stood directly beneath the Wyrm's pulsing glow. And when there was no more tower to scale, he would have jumped from the tower, trying to reach the egg, his thin arms outstretched, falling to his death. Meilin knew this was true because the courtyard around the tower was already thick with the broken bodies of those who had tried the very same thing. Sacrifices to the Wyrm.

Conor had been infected by one of the Wyrm's parasites in Nilo. He had fought bravely against the corroding power, but it was clear that his constitution was fading. When they first landed in this fallen Sadrean city, the home of the Wyrm, Conor had tried running toward the egg, fighting anyone who dared to get in his way, even his own spirit animal, Briggan. Meilin and Takoda had finally resorted to binding his hands and feet so he couldn't run. Briggan now lay beside Conor, curled up like a guard dog. Whether he was trying to protect Conor from the group or the group from Conor was unclear.

"We can't release you," Meilin said again. "Not until you're free of the Wyrm's control. It's for your own protection."

Conor grit his teeth, lurching as if a surge of pain had just slithered through his whole body. "Let me GO!" he growled. He jerked his arms and feet, pulling at his ropes, even though the struggle clearly caused him more pain.

Meilin set down her sponge and touched the tattoo on her arm. Jhi, the Great Panda, appeared at her side, yawning. Meilin reached out and scratched the black fur behind Jhi's ears. "Can you help him?" she whispered. "Can you stop the cuts on his arms and legs from getting infected?"

Jhi cast a doubtful look at the boy but nodded solemnly and lumbered toward Conor. Meilin noted with a pang of sympathy that Jhi's body looked thin, which was not a good look for a great panda. There had been little food beyond what mushrooms and roots the group could forage—and these were not things that Jhi enjoyed eating. Meilin tried to keep her in passive state as often as possible, but she also knew that Conor needed all the help he could get.

She watched as Jhi stepped around Briggan to Conor's side. The panda leaned down and licked the wounds around Conor's bound ankles.

"Get away from me!" Conor screamed, kicking his legs.

Jhi gave a sharp *yip* as Conor's foot struck her in the muzzle.

"Conor!" Meilin shouted, standing. She already had her fists out, ready to defend her spirit animal. Briggan had sprung to his feet and was crouched beside her, also growling at Conor.

Jhi turned toward both of them and shook her head, letting them know that she was unharmed. She turned back to Conor and again began ministering to the boy's wounds. Conor struggled but soon gave way to exhaustion and fell back asleep.

"Thanks," Meilin said, looking down at Briggan. "I know this can't be easy for you, either."

The wolf let out a quiet whine, his tail slunk down, and returned to Conor's feet.

THE FALLEN CITY

A FTER SUMMONING JHI BACK INTO PASSIVE STATE,
Meilin left Conor to visit the top deck of the lighthouse. A modest structure overlooked the shores of the
Sulfur Sea. This building, like everything else in the city,
was carved from some sort of rare stone that she had
never seen before. She found Takoda at the top of the
steps, seated at the open window.

"I heard shouts downstairs," Takoda said. "Conor?"

Meilin nodded, chewing at the inside of her cheek.
"He's asleep now. Jhi is tending to him." Kovo was
nowhere to be seen, which didn't surprise her. The Great
Beast spent most of his time maintaining the glowstone
perimeter that he had set up around the center of the
city. The Many were afraid of the light, and the glowstones created a barrier that protected them from
approaching the bell tower. Kovo was almost fanatical
about the glowstones. He spent every day maintaining
them, searching for new stones to replace those that had
begun to dim.

Meilin joined Takoda at the window, which overlooked the eastern half of the city. The lamp in the lighthouse was meant to be fueled by glowstones, which Kovo had taken away. In their stead he had stocked the lighthouse with clay urns of oil and medicine that he had gathered from apothecaries and abandoned shops around the city. He insisted that the urns remain untouched but when asked what they were for, he refused to explain.

Meilin, Conor, and Takoda had been traveling the caverns of Sadre for what must have been weeks now. Down here it was like a second world, one hidden beneath the surface of Erdas, populated by its own tribes and creatures. Meilin certainly missed the warmth of the sun, but what she missed most was the simple ability to count the days. In Sadre there were no days, only perpetual darkness—one endless night.

"You don't know how important sunlight is until it's gone," she said.

Takoda nodded slightly, his eyes fixed on the slightly phosphorescent waves lapping against the shore. "It's kind of peaceful, though," he said.

Meilin didn't know how to respond to this, and so she said nothing. She stared at the Sulfur Sea, which even from here emitted an unpleasant brimstone aroma. They had only barely escaped those dark waters.

In her mind, Meilin could still hear the piercing shriek of the corrupted eels that had nearly devoured her and her friends. She tried not to think of Teutar and the rest of the crew of the *Meleager*, who had sacrificed themselves so Meilin and her friends could continue their quest to stop the Wyrm.

And now, after so much struggle and pain, they had reached their destination: a fallen city that looked to be older than time. Giant stone towers connected by bridges and twisting staircases were chiseled right out of the strange rock.

"It must have been beautiful, don't you think? Before everything?" Takoda had asked the question upon landing on the shores of the city. Meilin noticed that Kovo had grimaced at his human partner—almost like a smile.

Even after all their travels, after all they had endured together, Meilin was still uncomfortable having the Great Ape in their party. He made no move to betray them, but she couldn't erase the memory of that final battle against Kovo at the Evertree. The gorilla was selfish, cruel, and, worst of all, he was smart. If it weren't for the fact that he alone seemed to have some sense of what was going on, she would have left Kovo behind a dozen times now.

Takoda had always argued that he thought Kovo's reasons for trying to take control of the Evertree were more complicated than *just* world domination. Now, seeing its roots firsthand, Meilin could only begrudgingly agree.

The city was located directly below the Evertree, whose silver roots spread across the cavernous ceiling, bathing the entire place in an eerie glow. And tangled in the roots of the tree was an enormous pulsing egg sack, tucked between the tendrils: the Wyrm.

Kovo had signed to Takoda that this place was called Hole, which was a strange name for a city. Meilin suspected that this was a bad translation. Then again, what did she know about these people or their naming customs? She had also noticed some carvings in the walls that seemed to be Hellan, which made sense. The Sadreans were descended, in more ways than one, from the ancient culture.

The Wyrm had not yet hatched, but Meilin could tell from the fractures in the egg's membrane that it would soon. The Evertree roots around the egg were starting to rot and fray—which also frayed Meilin's bond with Jhi. Even now, thousands of tiny wriggling parasites slithered from the cracks and fell to the ground far below. The same parasites that had spread all across Sadre, taking over any living thing they touched.

The people of Hole had long since been overwhelmed by the parasites. They were now what the Sadreans called the Many—shuffling, mindless drones enslaved to the will of the Wyrm. Meilin closed her eyes, thinking again of Conor. How much longer until he joined their ranks?

The streets were clogged with the Wyrm's wriggling parasites, and so they had been forced to make camp on higher ground in the lighthouse at the edge of the city. Takoda and Kovo had blocked all the lower entrances. It was a safe place, but they were still trapped. And eventually, the Many would find a way in. The Many always found a way in.

Meilin knew this because she had already seen it happen in the city of Phos Astos. The Many had overwhelmed the Sadreans who lived there and destroyed them. If it weren't for the actions of a brave girl named Xanthe, Meilin and her friends might have been among the casualties. Xanthe had led them away from the destruction—away from her own crumbling home—in order to find the Wyrm.

"I wish Xanthe was here," Takoda whispered, as if reading Meilin's thoughts. "I'll bet she knows a lot about this place."

Meilin bristled. The girl had been lost during a fiery race across the Arachane Fields—Xanthe had begged them not to set fire to the fields, but Takoda hadn't listened.

And now Xanthe was gone.

Takoda had taken the loss especially hard, and Meilin suspected that he secretly blamed himself for it. But blame aside, she knew that this was no time for mourning.

"*Knew*," Meilin said, more brusquely than she meant. "She *knew* about this place. She's gone, Takoda. The best thing you can do to honor her sacrifice is finish what we set out to do."

Takoda looked at her with his deep, dark eyes. "You don't know that she's dead," he said. "Not for sure."

"Maybe not," Meilin said. "But I *do* know that we need you here. This whole place is swarming with the Many, and that egg is on the verge of hatching. We can't have you pining at the window for your lost crush."

Takoda could never know it, but Meilin's words were just as much for herself as him. She, too, had left someone behind. Someone she desperately longed to see once more.

"This is war, Takoda. We have to behave like warriors."

Takoda narrowed his eyes. "You sound like Kovo. Besides, if you truly believed that, you would have left Conor behind."

"Conor got infected trying to save you!" Meilin said, stomping her foot. "Besides, he's a Greencloak. He's one of us."

"Greencloaks . . ." Takoda's face twisted with disgust. "You all think that having a spirit animal is what makes someone special," he said, his expression strained with emotion. "A spirit animal isn't a gift. It's a curse. It defines you before you have a chance to define yourself. After my parents died, the monastery was the only place I'd finally felt at peace. I was supposed to be a monk, to spend my life transcribing scrolls and ringing holy bells. Now I'm nothing but Kovo the Ape's human partner. A sidekick to a monster."

Takoda was usually so meek and conciliatory, but not now. His hands were clenched into tight fists at his side. He looked like he wanted to throttle something. It was clear he had been sitting on this well of anger for some time. "If I didn't have a spirit animal, I'd still be home with my brothers and sisters. And Xanthe would still be safe."

"There *is* no safe," Meilin said, softening her tone. "Not anymore." She remembered her own mighty empire of Zhong falling to waves of Conquerors. She remembered her father dying on the battlefield, his life snuffed out as she watched. "Your monastery would have been destroyed by the Many, or Zerif, or the Wyrm. Xanthe's city would have fallen even if we hadn't arrived. What threatens us now threatens all of Erdas. If you want to save Nilo and Phos Astos, then we have to destroy the Wyrm—quickly, before it can hatch."

She crouched down and began drawing a map of the city in the dusty floor with her finger. "I've been thinking: Maybe Kovo can help us salvage parts to build a siege engine. With a catapult we could launch some kind of missile at the egg. My father's armies used them to defend their fortresses. I think I can draw up plans." She knew doing such a thing would also damage the Evertree, but she thought it was worth the risk.

Takoda stepped back. "We've been through this already," he said firmly. "Kovo says we have to wait."

"Wait for *what*?" Meilin said, striking the ground with her hand. Ever since reaching the ruined city, there had been ongoing tension about how to destroy the Wyrm. Meilin knew they had to act, but Kovo—again and again—insisted that they not disturb the egg.

She stood up, meeting Takoda's eye. "The Wyrm is only going to get stronger. We've journeyed all this way, racing to get here before it hatches. And now we're supposed to just sit around and wait for it to do just that?"

"Yes."

Meilin threw up her arms. "If you hate Kovo so much, why are you taking his side?"

Takoda sighed. "I don't hate him. I wish I could, but my bond won't let me. And I—I can just tell that this is different. . . ." He shook his head, trying to describe something indescribable. "Kovo may hate humans, but he hates the Wyrm even more. He wants to stop it as much as anyone. When it's time to act, he'll let us know."

Meilin blew a strand of dark hair from her face. "And just when will that be? Because soon every person in Erdas will become infected by the Wyrm's parasites. What's happening to Conor downstairs will happen to all of us unless we *act*. Do you want that blood on your hands?"

Before Takoda could answer, there was a loud *whump* from the other end of the room. The impact was so great that it shook the floor beneath them.

Meilin turned to see Kovo had scaled the tower from outside, returning from his rounds. The Great Ape lumbered in through the window, eyes wide. He looked out of breath, like he had raced clear across the city to reach them.

"What's got you all worked up?" she said.

The ape ignored her, staggering closer. He placed an enormous black hand on Takoda's shoulder. The moment he made contact with his human partner, the boy gasped, as if the very breath had been pulled from his lungs.

"I . . . I . . ." the boy said, his voice hollow and strange.

Meilin stared at Takoda's dark eyes, which had changed to a shimmering, iridescent color—like the inside of an oyster shell. She saw now that Kovo's eyes were likewise transformed.

"Takoda?" Meilin said. "What did he do to you?"

The boy turned toward her, blinking his swirling eyes.

"I have a message from Abeke and Rollan."

VOICE FROM AFAR

M EILIN STARED AT TAKODA AND KOVO, BOTH OF THEM opal-eyed and unblinking. "You have . . . what?" she asked.

Takoda tilted his head, as if trying to hear a faint sound. "Someone named Shane is with them."

Meilin nearly choked on her spit. "*Shane?* The same Shane who tried to conquer the world?" If Shane was with them, it could only mean that they were in trouble.

Takoda shrugged, shaking his head. "I'm just the messenger," he said. "I actually don't really understand what's happening."

Kovo grunted and made a gesture to Takoda with one hand. The boy nodded and turned back to Meilin. "Kovo says it's him. I . . . I think he's trying to help. He's been working to keep the Great Beasts from Zerif, just like your friends. He's trying to make up for past sins."

Meilin narrowed her eyes. "He told you *all that* with just a flick of his wrist?" She knew that Kovo and

Takoda had devised a way of communicating through gestures, but this seemed different.

Takoda shrugged again. "He didn't have to say it. I just . . . *knew*." Takoda seemed as genuinely confused by all this as she was. "It's like I can hear different voices in my head. Kovo . . . and a girl I don't know, and one more . . . Mulop?"

"Mulop?" Meilin said. Something like comprehension began to dawn on her. "The Great Beast?" She took a trembling breath. It was obvious that *something* strange was happening to Kovo and Takoda, even if she couldn't tell what. She didn't trust it. For all she knew, this was another plot by Shane, or perhaps some new effect of the Wyrm. "How are they contacting us?" she said carefully.

"How are you contacting us?" Takoda repeated. He cast his ear to the air and responded a moment later. "Mulop has linked minds with Kovo . . . but the connection will not last very long. We are . . . very far away, and Mulop's powers are weak." Takoda's voice was stilted, as though he were carefully repeating something that was being dictated to him. "Where are you?"

"I'm not sure we can tell them that," Meilin said, inching back. "How do we know we can trust you?"

Takoda repeated her question and then listened for the answer. He snorted slightly before saying, "Rollan would like me to ask Jhi what it's like being bonded to a snotty general's daughter. Also, he wants to know if stubbornness is a skill you picked up from your fancy tutors."

A smile spread across Meilin's face. "That's Rollan, all right." She hoped that neither Takoda nor Kovo could hear the catch in her voice or see her blushing. "Fine," she said, regaining her composure. "What do you need to know?"

KOVO SPEAKS

ROLLAN STOOD NEXT TO ABEKE AND SHANE IN THE cold cavern, shivering. Drops of water ran down icy stalactites and splashed on the wet floor in small puddles. Before him sat Niri, her legs dangling in the steaming water. The girl's eyes swirled with a rainbow of colors, her blue-inked fingers clutching Mulop's tentacle.

It had worked. They were *actually* talking to Meilin. Which meant Meilin was *alive*. A thousand questions churned around in Rollan's mind as he tried to decide what to ask.

But before Rollan could say anything, Shane spoke up. "What can Kovo tell us about the Wyrm? Does he know how to stop it?"

Rollan gritted his teeth. "Why does *he* get to do all the talking?"

Abeke put a calming hand on his arm. "If it weren't for Shane, we wouldn't be here at all."

Niri asked Shane's question. After a moment, she began speaking for Kovo. It was her voice, but the phrasing and tone sounded different—like she was channeling Kovo's cold growl with every word.

"Aeons ago, the Wyrm's egg fell from the stars," she began, "like a stone plunging into a pool. It was a time before humans fouled the soil with their presence." The girl screwed up her mouth, as if trying to find a word. "Things were *quiet*. Still. The world was golden and blue. . . . Beasts lived alongside one another in harmony—fed by the Evertree. Spirit animals didn't exist. Neither did the Great Beasts."

Rollan had trouble imagining a world without humans or spirit animals or Great Beasts. The thought of a world without Essix saddened him.

"In those ancient days," Niri continued, "the continents were a single mass that covered half the world. Mountains and deserts and snow were all together in this place—all of Erdas's wonders in a single room. When the Wyrm's egg struck the earth, the impact was so great that the land shattered into pieces, floating apart from one another."

"So a falling egg *shattered* the world?" Rollan muttered, with not a small amount of skepticism. "In my experience, that's not what happens when eggs hit the ground."

Niri shook her head, clarifying in her own voice. "I don't think it was an ordinary egg. Its shell was made from a rock stronger than anything on Erdas." A moment later, she continued speaking for Kovo. "The Wyrm was drawn to the Evertree—it could sense the life coursing through its branches. When the Wyrm landed, it caused great destruction—storms, floods, and earthquakes—that wiped out nearly every living thing for miles. Only fifteen creatures survived—sheltered from death by the branches of the Evertree."

"The Great Beasts . . ." Abeke whispered. "That's why you know all this. You were *there*."

Rollan shot a look over to the girl. Abeke's eyes were wide with wonder. "So, you're telling us that the Wyrm somehow *created* the Great Beasts," he said slowly.

"Yes," said Niri after a moment. "Our peaceful lives were over. Everything we knew and loved had been destroyed. We fifteen beasts were all that remained. But worst of all was what the Wyrm did to the tree itself. The Evertree survived the impact, but it was different."

"Different *how*?" Rollan said.

"The tree no longer gave mere life. It did something more dangerous—it forged an invisible bond that flowed between living things." She paused a moment to let these words sink in. "The Evertree is the source of the spirit animal bond. And the Wyrm is the source of that power. Everything leads back to *it*."

"You're telling us that it's the *Wyrm* that created the spirit animal bond," Rollan said, and this time there was no skepticism in his voice. "Why would it do that?"

"The same reason all creatures do what they do," Niri said for Kovo. "Because it is *hungry*."

"I don't buy it." Rollan waved his hands, interrupting Niri. "If the Wyrm created spirit animal bonds, then it's *good*. Isn't it? Why would an evil creature bring life? That doesn't make any sense."

"It's a good question," Shane said.

Niri asked the question aloud and then gave Kovo's response. "The Wyrm is a parasite that feeds on life itself. And like any parasite, it is both hungry . . . and patient. In order to feed, it needs two things. First, a food source. Thanks to the Evertree, it now has that in abundance. Second, it needs a host in order to fully mature. Once hatched, it will bond itself to that host—and then it will be unstoppable. For centuries, it has been waiting for a creature strong enough to contain it. And for just as long, *I alone* have been working to stop it."

"Kovo the long-suffering hero?" Rollan threw his hands up. "I thought Yumaris was crazy, but this takes the cake."

"Impudent human!" Niri's lips curled suddenly into a snarl. All at once, Rollan could see Kovo's scowling face peering out through the girl's features.

"Niri?" Shane asked, stepping tentatively forward.

"*I alone* sensed the Wyrm's hunger," Niri growled, her voice thick with contempt—she wasn't just translating for Kovo anymore; it was like he was speaking directly through her. "The weakness twisting beneath the world. The corruption that fueled *every* spirit animal bond. My war against the Greencloaks was a war against *the Wyrm*—for only my brethren and I could possibly contain its power."

Niri was practically spitting now, her face a mask of fury. Her gleaming opal eyes flared red. "My first attempt to destroy it with the Hellans failed. Human civilizations are castles made of sand—easily washed away. So I took matters into my own hands. I would gather the talismans and wrest control of the Evertree, by force if necessary. Better a thousand kingdoms fall than the Wyrm should claim its host. Better my siblings *die* than become slaves to such a *thing*."

Rollan glimpsed Shane, who was watching the girl with his mouth agape. Rollan felt a rare twist of sympathy for the fallen monarch. *Shane's* kingdom had been one of those thousands that Kovo was so willing to sacrifice.

He also felt confusion. Rollan tried to consider what was being said—that Kovo's wicked plotting had all been in defense of Erdas—but he couldn't believe it. Kovo had killed too many, had destroyed too much, to ever be *good*.

"Once the Evertree was destroyed," Niri continued, her face softening, "its grip on the Wyrm loosened. The Wyrm grew restless. It will wait no longer. Through its parasites, the Wyrm is creating its *own* perfect host. Someone more powerful than all the Great Beasts combined."

"Zerif," Abeke said. A silence shivered through the cavern. The thought of an even more powerful version of Zerif—one bonded with an aeons-old malevolent Wyrm—was too frightening to contemplate.

"This all sounds nice, but it's just a theory," Rollan said. "If the egg isn't hatched, how does Kovo know what the Wyrm is planning?"

"He's telling the truth about Zerif," Shane said. "Mulop has been peering inside Zerif's mind. Zerif thinks he's in control, but he's being manipulated, just like all of the infected."

Niri swallowed, her face trembling from the strain of the connection. Drops of sweat fell from her hair. "The Wyrm is waiting until Zerif has gathered enough power," she said slowly, "and then it will break free from its egg and find him. Once they're bonded, nothing will be able to stop it from consuming the world."

"We know these ruins are some sort of trap that Kovo helped the Hellans build," Shane said. "We need to know how to trigger the trap. How do we stop the Wyrm from hatching and bonding with Zerif?"

Niri frowned, her breath coming in ragged gasps. "How do we stop the Wyrm?" she said. She turned her head, as though she were having trouble hearing the response. When she spoke, her words were halting. "The . . . only way to trigger . . . the snare . . ." She interrupted herself with a sharp gasp. Mulop's tentacle slipped from her grip, sliding back into the pool of water. Niri fell backward, her body limp.

"The only way is *what*?" Shane cried, running toward Niri, who had slumped over on the rock. He grabbed her by the shoulders, shaking her. "How do we trigger the snare?"

"It looks like our little chat is over," Rollan said, noting that he could no longer see Mulop's shadowy form on the other side of the icy wall.

Niri turned her head toward Shane, blinking. Her eyes had returned to normal, and her face was pale from fright. "Zerif," she whispered. "He's found us."

HALF A PLAN

MEILIN STOOD IN THE DARKENED LIGHTHOUSE, staring at Takoda, whose eyes had returned to their normal brown color. Both he and Kovo looked like they were recovering from a bout of particularly bad nausea.

"Are you okay?" Meilin asked, grabbing the boy by the arm so he didn't tumble out the open window.

Takoda ran a trembling hand through his dark hair. "Just dizzy," he said. "I had four separate voices echoing in my head. It was hard to make sense of it all." His eyes flashed to Kovo, who seemed to have become very interested in the view out the window.

"Well, just take a moment to catch your breath," Meilin said. "Jhi can help with the nausea." And so saying, she summoned Jhi, who immediately toddled to Takoda's side and began nuzzling a place on the boy's temple.

Kovo remained where he stood, but his bearing was altogether less fierce than it had been half an hour before. It was clear that his little tirade had drained him.

The ape reached out a giant hand and patted Takoda on the shoulder in a way that alarmed Meilin for its gentleness. Perhaps their little conversation had changed the way Takoda and Kovo felt about each other. She glanced at Jhi, following the panda as she worked. Meilin wondered what it would be like to truly inhabit the mind of her spirit animal. A part of her feared what she would learn if she could hear Jhi's true opinion of her.

"Do you know why the connection was cut short?" she asked after Takoda had more fully recovered. "What happened to Abeke and Rollan?"

Takoda swallowed. "I don't know. . . . Mulop couldn't maintain the connection. Something pulled his attention away. I could feel it, too, for a heartbeat— the thing that interrupted him. I could sense something approaching."

Kovo nodded, making a sign that she recognized as "danger."

"Zerif," Meilin said, stepping back. "He must have found them." She closed her fists tight, wishing she could fight alongside her friends. She didn't know what to make of the fact that Shane was with them now, but she hoped the former Conqueror could protect Abeke and Rollan in the coming battle.

Meilin shook these fears from her mind. They had a mission to complete, and she couldn't let herself get distracted. "We have to destroy the Wyrm before it can hatch and bond with Zerif," she said. "Let's get started."

"I don't think we can kill the Wyrm before it hatches," Takoda said. "The only thing that can get through that egg is the Wyrm itself. It would have hatched already, if it weren't for those roots binding it tight—the tree is trying to save us all."

"But I thought the Evertree was part of the Wyrm's evil plan?" She was still struggling to process this new idea that the spirit bond was really the product of the Wyrm. "The tree is a puppet, just like the rest of us."

"Maybe so," Takoda said. "But maybe, like us, the Evertree knows what it means for the Wyrm to hatch. Just like we're fighting against its power, so is the tree."

Meilin cast a sidelong glance at the boy. She didn't know how things went in southern Nilo, but in Zhong, people didn't believe that plants had feelings. "If the Evertree can't stop it, then how do we?"

Takoda eyed the ceiling. "It's like the Sadrean elders told us in Phos Astos. Kovo helped the ancient Hellans build this place to stop the Wyrm."

"I remember," Meilin said. "They said he constructed some kind of secret weapon." She turned to the gorilla. "So where is this weapon?"

The ape snorted and then made a gesture.

"We're standing in it," Takoda explained. "The city *is* the trap."

"Great," Meilin said. "So all we have to do is set it off. How do we do that?"

"Kovo won't say. Even though I could see inside Kovo's mind, hear his thoughts, it was clear that he wanted to keep that knowledge hidden." The boy touched the handle of an enormous iron mallet propped against the wall. Kovo had found the mallet on their first day in the city and now kept it with him always. "I think it has something to do with this mallet."

Kovo turned, glaring at them both and snarling. He marched over to Takoda and snatched the mallet from the boy, as though it weighed no more than a twig. He obviously wanted to cut short their speculation about how this trap might actually work.

"This is no time for secrets," Meilin said, following after the gorilla. "If you know something, you have to tell us."

"Don't judge him too harshly," Takoda said. "He's guarded this place for centuries. I think he's afraid of one of us becoming infected by the Wyrm's parasites and betraying our plan."

"As if *we're* the ones who can't be trusted," Meilin said, folding her arms. "Speaking of traps, this feels an awful lot like we're walking into one."

She recalled with a flash of rage the way Kovo had manipulated and used humans, animals, and even his fellow Great Beasts. How he had raised up an army of Conquerors to destroy the Greencloaks. "Who's to say Kovo's not just plotting to take control of the Wyrm and harness its power for himself? It wouldn't be the first time he's tried it."

The gorilla gave a low, dangerous growl, his black hands tensed around the mallet as though he might be considering its use on her skull.

"Stop!" Takoda said, pushing himself between them. "Kovo is not the enemy."

"Not the enemy?" Meilin actually laughed aloud. "Tell that to the legions of Greencloaks who died trying to protect Erdas. Tell that to Tarik, and Barlow, and *my father.*"

"And *my* family . . ." Takoda said. "You're not the only one who's lost something." He looked back at the gorilla, his expression torn between anger and empathy. "I know Kovo's done wicked things. But he's fighting a bigger war—one older than the Greencloaks. Kovo is no friend of humanity, but we all share a common enemy in the Wyrm. And he's sacrificed more than any of us in order to stop it. We have to trust him."

Meilin could not believe what she was hearing. "An hour ago, you hated Kovo as much as anyone—now suddenly he's your best friend?"

Takoda frowned. "The Kovo you battled at the Evertree is gone. When I summoned him as a spirit animal, he had no choice but to see the world through human eyes—at least a little bit. You don't have to trust him, but you should trust me." Takoda stared at her, his eyes wide and pleading. "What do you say?"

Meilin eyed the iron mallet clasped in the gorilla's huge hand. "So it has something to do with that mallet. What are we supposed to do with it? Whack the Wyrm on the head?" Her gaze moved past Kovo toward the window, which looked out into the center of the city.

Which looked out to the bell tower.

It really was an enormous structure. Its base was covered with pillars and round platforms. In the dim light, they almost looked like stone cogs and pistons—parts of some ancient machine.

"The bell tower," she said. "That's the trigger for the weapon, isn't it?"

Kovo blinked, his face screwed up. He looked annoyed, but not at her. After a moment, he made a few hand gestures, which Takoda was able to translate.

"It is not a weapon like you're thinking. It's more like a trap . . . and even that word isn't quite right. He keeps talking about the tides. . . ."

"So we're meant to *drown* the Wyrm?" Meilin said, struggling to follow. "I'd think a creature able to destroy all of Erdas could swim."

Kovo shook his great head and gestured again, growing more frustrated.

"That's not right, either," Takoda said. "It's . . . it's Erdas. Erdas will stop the Wyrm." Takoda shook his head, struggling to keep apace with Kovo's gestures. "It's too complicated to explain. But I think I know how these ruins are meant to work." He pointed out the window. "There are two towers—one here, and the other where your friends are—and they're connected by a tunnel that runs right through the heart of Erdas. When the bell is rung, the towers will be activated and the trap will be set into motion."

Meilin nodded vaguely. "So we need to ring the bell to spring the trap?" She looked out the window toward the middle of the city, at the bell tower that rose above the rest of the buildings. "That explains why Kovo was so eager to protect the tower from the Many. He must have been afraid that the Many climbing all over it would damage the bell."

Kovo nodded and made more gestures to his human partner.

Takoda watched, his eyes following the quickly moving hands. It seemed to Meilin that since communing with Kovo through Mulop, the boy was better at understanding his spirit animal's gestures. "Until the Wyrm hatches," Takoda said, "it's our job to protect that tower from the Many. If the Wyrm learns of our plan ahead of time, it might try to destroy the tower before it can be activated."

Meilin leaned against a giant urn of spiced truffle oil and blew a strand of hair from her face. "Let's just hope we don't die of hunger before the moment arrives. Or boredom." Waiting might have been something a monk like Takoda could do, but Meilin was a warrior, a person of action. She felt Jhi place an understanding paw on her foot. The panda, it seemed, knew Meilin's discomfort.

She heard a sharp bark as Briggan appeared at the top of the stairs. The wolf had remained with Conor below for the conversation, but was now pawing at the floor, whining.

"Something's wrong," Takoda said, already moving. "I think he wants us to go downstairs."

Meilin grabbed her staff and followed after them. Briggan was growling, and his fur had bristled along his back—he looked frightened. As soon as Meilin reached the bottom of the stairs, she saw why.

In the corner of the room was a pile of worn rope.

And no Conor.

"Conor," she said, her heart pounding in her ear. "He's gone."

Takoda, Kovo, and Jhi were soon at her side. They looked in every corner of the room and double-checked the door, which was still barred from the inside.

"He must have climbed out through the window," she said, peering out into the streets below. "If he survived the fall."

"Have you noticed something else?" Takoda said, standing beside her. "The streets—they've all gone dark."

Takoda was right. The barrier of glowstones that they had placed around the perimeter had all been extinguished.

"And if the lights are out," Meilin said, "then the Many could be anywhere."

Meilin inched back from the window as she heard a gargling hiss from just outside. The pale hand of what might have once been a woman appeared on the open sill, her fingernails cracked and black. The creature reached up another hand and pulled herself over the windowsill, peering into the darkness. She snarled at Meilin and Takoda.

Meilin already had her quarterstaff in her hand, and she swung it at the woman with such force that her head snapped back with a violent jerk. The creature snarled and gave a choked howl as her body fell from the window and plummeted to the ground below.

Meilin and Takoda raced back to the window, peering down to the streets. In the glowing light of the Evertree, they could just make out the broken body of the creature, dragging herself along the pavement.

"We need light," Meilin said, and ran to the bag that they'd managed to salvage from the *Meleager*. Inside was a small ball resembling a soft nut—one of only three they had left. Meilin hurled the nut out the open window onto the street below. The ball struck the ground and splattered phosphorescent milky goo in every direction. Eerie pinkish light filled the street, and in that light they could see dozens of the Many teeming in the streets, climbing on top of one another, all moving toward the bell tower.

The Many snarled, recoiling from the flash of light, which was already beginning to fade. Meilin stared at their hideous faces, skin drawn tight on their sharp bones. On each forehead she could see the rotting purple spiral of the parasite that had infected them. The Many were all bald, and their clothes, if they had any, were rotted rags.

All but one of them, who moved at the front of the line. His yellow hair looked dark in the shadows, and over his shoulders hung a tattered green cloak. Unlike the others, who howled and hid from the glowstone, he marched right to the light and, removing his cloak, laid the fabric over the splattered goo, dimming it so the others could continue their charge toward the Wyrm. The boy remained where he was, staring up at the lighthouse—staring straight at Meilin.

Briggan gave a sharp whine, pushing his muzzle into Meilin's sleeve. She stared at the boy below, whose figure was now only the ghost of a shadow. But even that glimpse had been long enough to confirm her fear.

"Conor," she said, stepping back, her heart throbbing in her chest. "He's raised an army against us."

MARCH OF THE MANY

C ONOR DIDN'T REMEMBER HOW HE HAD MANAGED TO escape his bonds in the lighthouse. Judging from the throbbing pain running up his arm, he thought he must have dislocated a thumb in the process.

The pain, however, didn't matter. Nor did the hunger gnawing in his stomach. Or the cold chill of the air without his cloak.

All that mattered was the Wyrm.

Conor had to reach the city square. He knew something, something about the bell tower in the middle of the city. Something about it was a threat to the Wyrm. He didn't understand how he knew this. He only knew that anything that tried to stop him would fall at his hand.

This would be a difficult journey—something or someone might try to stop him. For that reason, he had taken pains to extinguish the glowstone lamps set throughout the city. The light bothered his eyes, but not nearly as much as the others, who were burned by the light as though by fire. He knew that if he could darken those lights, he would soon have a legion at his side.

And so it was. No sooner had the first glowstone been shattered than he could sense his brethren skittering out from the shadows to join him. He could hear their heartbeats, beating with his own—steady and strong. He could see that they suffered just as he did—they were tormented with their desire to follow the Wyrm's command. And he could help lead them.

They were all children of the Wyrm.

Truly, it was a feeling of peace. The calm that comes from one finally accepting his place in the world. His whole life, Conor had been torn between duty and desire—always playing the meek shepherd, even when he wanted so much more. And now, at last, the Wyrm had called to him, had chosen *him*. And with that call came a promise of something so powerful, so pure, that he knew he would die if he could not touch it.

But even as he staggered over the cracked stone streets, moving toward the middle of the city, he felt another pull. He had a vague unease echoing in the deepest parts of his mind. A mournful baying—like the howling of a wolf—that seemed to tell him that what he was doing was wrong. That the Wyrm was dangerous. That he had to stop it before it was too late.

But that sound was faint in comparison to his own throbbing heart, which beat like a drum, compelling him to march forward. Conor's dark eyes slid to the hundreds of others walking beside him. How could so many souls be wrong? And when he finally reached the Wyrm, he knew that voice would be silenced at last.

"Conor!" a voice cried out in the darkness before him. It was not a voice in his head, but a real voice. It was the voice of a girl.

There was a flash of wincing light, which sent the others into hiding. Conor remained where he was. The light revealed their path—the path that led directly to the bell tower in the middle of the city—and it was blocked by two children and three beasts. The girl who had called to him was standing in the middle of the group. She wore a green cloak and held a long staff. Conor thought her name might be Meilin, and then he wondered how he knew that.

"Conor," the girl said, her body crouched like one preparing to fight. "You have to stop. You don't know what you're doing. You're being controlled by the Wyrm. You need to resist its power."

Conor felt his entire body flood with nauseous hatred as he recalled who these people were. These were interlopers. His former friends, who had held him captive in the tower, tied at the wrists and ankles. They had tried to keep him from the Wyrm. And now they were blocking his path.

These are my enemiessss, a voice said in his mind. It was a deep, pulsing voice that seemed to reverberate through his very bones. A voice that spoke without actual words in a language even older than the stars. A voice of limitless power.

Protecttt meee, the voice said.

Protecttt meee, and killll them.

13

URNS

MEILIN HAD NO REAL WAY OF KNOWING HOW TO STOP what was coming. They were two children and three spirit animals against an army of hundreds—maybe even thousands. The last time they had encountered the Many in Phos Astos, they had barely escaped with their lives. And now they were somehow supposed to defeat them in battle, with one of her closest friends leading the opposite charge.

She stared at Conor shuffling toward her, his lifeless eyes glossy and dark. The boy she knew was barely recognizable.

"Conor!" she called again. "You have to fight the Wyrm! Resist its call!"

If Conor heard her plea, it did not show on his face. That was perhaps a blessing. Conor had fought countless battles at Meilin's side. He knew her weaknesses as a fighter, and he could certainly exploit them. Already he had shown himself cunning enough to extinguish the lights around the main square—enabling the Many to come to his side.

She wondered whether he had overheard any of their conversation at the lighthouse. How much did he know about Kovo's plan? And if Conor knew, did the Wyrm know as well?

Meilin felt a shiver in the air that made the hair on the back of her neck stand up. Briggan whined, his hackles raised, as though hearing the cry of an unheard song. Jhi, who was beside Meilin, seemed similarly agitated.

The Many had also stopped their approach, all of them tilting their heads up toward the Wyrm, which pulsed above the city like an oozing black sun.

"What's happening?" Meilin said, adjusting her grip on her staff. "Why did they all stop?"

Kovo made a gesture beside her, which Takoda translated. "The Wyrm," the boy said. "It's speaking to them."

She stared overhead at the pulsing polyp that was the Wyrm's egg. Through the crack in its shell, she could see a red light glowing. The red light opened, like an eye, rolling back and forth and blinking. The egg shuddered, as if whatever was inside was struggling to break free.

"It's waking up," Meilin said.

The Many, all of whom had been distracted by the Wyrm's movement, turned their attention back to the street. Their pale faces were twisted with animal hatred. Conor raised a thin finger, pointing toward Meilin. With a hideous, inhuman roar, the Many rushed past him and charged toward Meilin and Takoda, hands outstretched like claws.

Briggan bared his teeth, growling. Even Jhi seemed ready to head-butt whoever might approach.

Meilin knelt low, preparing for the first assault. She grunted, swinging her staff upward with a jaw-breaking *crack* against the face of her first opponent—a man in the ragged robes of a Sadrean elder. The man flew backward, falling to the ground.

With so many coming, there was hardly time to breathe, let alone change footing. Meilin brought her staff down without pausing, bashing a Sadrean boy who looked even younger than Takoda. A moment later, both the boy and the elder were trampled under the feet of the Many who had taken their place.

Takoda fought beside her with more passion than skill. In a surprising display of strength, he swung Kovo's iron mallet over his head and brought it down with a terrible *crunch*. The mallet weighed nearly as much as the boy, and his swing was strong enough to topple a trio of the Many, who flew backward, unconscious.

Briggan had managed to fell half a dozen already. Meilin could not take time to note whether or not the injuries the wolf inflicted with his jaws were fatal. Nor could she contemplate how she might feel if they were.

Meilin rolled across the ground, knocking out a man who very nearly managed to grab Takoda from behind. She felt a slithering sense of horror as she realized that one of the Wyrm's parasites had managed to attach itself to her neck. She ripped the thing off and flung it into the shadows.

"Get to higher ground!" she called out, springing to her feet. "We need to rekindle those glowstones and keep them at bay." She leaped backward to some fallen rubble on the blockade.

Jhi, meanwhile, had taken it upon herself to amble directly into the fray and lead off a faction of the Many, who pursued the panda with blind fury. Meilin watched from her new height as Jhi led them straight off the edge of a rocky ledge that opened into a deep well below. Dozens of the Many followed Jhi into the water, sputtering and splashing to keep from drowning.

Meilin grinned and touched her arm. A moment later, Jhi's mark appeared on her flesh. She pressed it again and Jhi appeared at her side, soaking wet and looking quite proud. "Nice work!" she said. "Care to try it again?" Jhi scrambled down from the barrier to lead off another group of the Many. Meilin watched her spirit animal rush headlong into danger, marveling at how she could have ever doubted the Great Panda's courage.

Meilin kicked her boot at the hand of a grasping man who looked like he was some kind of warrior. She brought her staff down on another, a woman who might have been beautiful if she hadn't been pale and hairless.

The Many were not strong, but they fought with absolutely no regard to personal safety, which made them relentless in their assault. However many Meilin knocked down, twice that number appeared a moment later. The fight was made even more difficult by the fact that the only light available was from the silvery roots of the Evertree. Meilin was battling an army of shadows.

"How are those glowstones coming?" Meilin shouted to Takoda, who was somewhere behind her.

"Gone!" he cried. "Conor shattered them all. We're out of light."

"That's just perfect!" Meilin said, ducking as Briggan leaped over her head to attack an approaching Sadrean. She recalled that Jhi was somewhere in the city, having led off another group of the Many. She had forgotten all about her! When she summoned Jhi into passive state, and then to her side, she saw that the panda's right haunch was red with blood. "Stay close to me," she whispered. "You've done more than enough."

Meilin scanned the slack faces before her, looking for Conor. Searching farther down the street, she saw that the boy had not charged the barrier with the others but had instead climbed up to the top of a small footbridge.

From there, he was now directing the rest of the Many like a general—pointing straight at the bell tower.

"Conor's leading an assault against the tower!" she called. "We have to stop him."

Meilin wished she had the ability to throw something far enough to knock Conor from his perch. She looked around for Kovo, but the gorilla was nowhere to be found.

"Takoda!" she cried. "Can you summon Kovo? We could really use an extra pair of fists right about now!" Kovo had single-handedly fought back the Many at Phos Astos.

"I'm trying, but it's not working!" Takoda shouted, wrenching his mallet free from a man who had grabbed hold of the handle. "He ran inside the lighthouse, telling me to seek shelter!"

"Seek shelter?" Meilin said, taking out a pale-faced old woman with a roundhouse kick. "Now's not really the time for retreat!" Even as she said this, she could feel Jhi's muzzle on her side, pushing her backward toward one of the crevices in their stone barricade. "What are you doing?!" she shouted, tripping over the back of her cloak and falling onto flat stone.

But then, up above her, she saw a dark figure standing atop the roof of the lighthouse. It was Kovo, and he was holding an enormous clay urn over his head—one of dozens that he had been collecting from all across the city over the last few days. A curl of black smoke leaked out from the mouth of the jar.

"Get back!" Meilin cried, her eyes widening.

With an earthshaking roar, the Great Gorilla hurled the urn toward the street below. It struck the ground with a crash as it burst into a ball of red flames.

The Many howled in pain at both the light and the heat as the fire raged in the street—scattering them in all directions. But Meilin's sense of triumph was over as soon as it had sparked when she looked to the bridge where Conor had been standing only a moment before—now a pile of burning rubble.

Briggan whined beside her and made to leap into the flames. Meilin grabbed his scruff, stopping him from finding his human companion. "You can't!" she cried. "We need you here."

The ruined city echoed with the moans of the Many as they scrambled to reach the shore and douse the flames that had engulfed their bodies. Already Kovo had raised another urn over his head. It came down with an explosion even bigger than the last, sending the horde even farther back.

Meilin scrambled to her feet, feeling a new hope swelling in her breast. There were at least twenty urns of oil in their tower—enough to build a flaming barrier around the middle of the city. That might at least buy them time to rest and recover, until they formed a new plan.

"We need to use the flames to create a perimeter around the bell tower—to cut them off from approaching." She turned to Takoda. "Run. Tell Kovo to throw one urn at every major inroad."

Her hope in victory, however, was short-lived. Meilin heard a snarl at her feet, and she glanced down just in time to see a black hand burst from the rubble and grab her ankle. "Ahhh!" she cried, as the hand pulled her toward the flames below. Meilin grabbed her staff and brought it down—so hard that it snapped in half against her attacker's head. Her assailant, however, was undeterred. He grabbed her with his other hand, pulling her closer to the consuming flames. And when Meilin looked upon his face, the fight went out of her.

"Conor," she whispered, for indeed it was. He stared at her with his dead-dark eyes, his skin charred and burned. The parasite burrowed into his brow was pulsing—it throbbed just beneath the skin like a second heart.

With a roar, Conor flung Meilin aside—showing more strength than she knew him to possess. It must have been the power of the Wyrm coursing through his veins.

Briggan growled and charged Conor, biting down on the boy's leg and pulling him away from Meilin. Conor stumbled down to his knees without crying out, kicking and fighting to get free of the wolf's jaws. But the damage had already been done. With Meilin and Briggan so distracted, there was nothing to stop the charge of the Many clambering up and over the flaming barricade. Despite the excruciating pain of the flames, these mindless captives were undeterred, using their own bodies to smother the fire so that those behind them might continue their assault.

Meilin felt Jhi beside her, tending to the burns on her leg where Conor had grabbed her. She watched, helpless, as hundreds of the Many charged straight through the flames, flowing into the center of the city.

Kovo hurled more urns in a desperate bid to stop them from reaching the spire, but it was useless. The Many cared not for their lives. They clawed at stones and bricks and bannisters—trying to rip the bell tower apart with their bare hands.

"It's over." Meilin felt the sting of smoke in her eyes as she blinked away hot tears. They had traveled all this way, sacrificed so much, only to fail in their task. And in that failure would come the destruction of all of Erdas. She clung to Jhi, burying her face in the panda's warm fur. "There's just too many of them."

"Well then," said a voice beside her, "maybe we should even the odds?" Meilin looked up to see Takoda, who, despite being covered with bruises and burns, was breathless and wide-cyed. "I think our prayers have been answered."

Before Meilin could ask him what he meant, she heard a shrill whining sound out in the distance. It was coming from the direction of the water. Meilin stood, recalling that piercing cry, which she had only heard twice before, while defending the walls of Phos Astos from the Many.

"Screamers," she said, speaking the name of the peculiar mushrooms that the Sadreans had used to defend their perimeters.

The sound was even louder now, so loud that the Many took leave of their work in the city square and turned toward the water—from which direction shone a dazzling pinkish light that cut sharp shadows across the streets. Meilin stood and shielded her eyes from the glare. At the water, she could see a dozen galley ships riding the dark waves to shore—all of them bearing enormous glowstones at the helm to light their paths. On the decks stood dozens of Sadrean soldiers, all of them wearing glittering crystalline armor and holding crystal swords and axes.

Even at this distance, Meilin could see the glint of determination burning in their pink eyes. And there, at the front of the prow, the small figure of a girl bearing a long spear. The girl's face was hidden behind a crystal helm, but Meilin could see clearly enough the glowing paw print showing on the breast of her tunic—a mark that Kovo himself had given her after their first battle in Phos Astos. "It can't be," Meilin whispered.

"It's her," Takoda said, the smile nearly splitting his face. "It's Xanthe."

XANTHE RETURNS

HAVING BEEN RAISED IN A MONASTERY, TAKODA HAD been taught to see tiny miracles in the world. But these were always small things. A rainbow cast off the glint of a dewy spiderweb. The first cry of a newborn babe. The music of a stream as it rippled by.

In this moment, however, as Takoda looked out past the rippling flames and saw Xanthe's face approaching from the sea, he finally understood what it was to behold a *real* miracle.

"She's alive," he said, barely able to form the words.

"And more important," Meilin said, standing beside him, "she's brought an army!"

Already the ships had reached the shore, and soldiers were racing down the gangplanks and into the city streets, weapons raised. The Many had greater numbers, but the Sadreans were well-armored and fierce. They fought with the might of a population that had survived the crucible of battle, only to emerge with newly forged strength. Xanthe herself fought as bravely as any of them, using her crystal spear to impale the Many who got in her way.

"Xanthe!" Takoda shouted, running to the top of a smoldering staircase and waving both arms over his head. "Over here!"

Xanthe turned her head and saw him. The girl's face broke into an astonished smile. There was a glint in her pink eyes that made Takoda's heart beat out of his chest. "You're alive!" she shouted, racing to meet him.

"I can't believe you found us!" he exclaimed. "How did you survive the Webmother?"

Xanthe shrugged. "I'm a Sadrean wanderling. Surviving the tunnels is what I do best." She was breathing hard from the fighting. "Besides," she said, looking down to the ground, "I thought you might miss me."

Takoda's mouth fell open. He didn't know what to say in response. There was something about the way Xanthe had said this that made him think maybe she felt the same way about him as he felt about her. "I . . . um . . ." He swallowed, his cheeks flushing.

Takoda was saved, as it were, by an interruption in the form of a loud crash. The battle was still raging around them, and hundreds of the Many had broken through the flames and were now scaling the side of the bell tower, tearing at the stonework and buttressing. They had just succeeded in breaking the masonry around one of the tower's lower turrets, which had fallen free from the main tower and crashed to the ground.

A huge cloud of dust filled the air. Takoda coughed, reaching out a hand to steady himself. His fingers found what he realized too late was Xanthe's hand. "S-sorry!" he stammered, pulling away. "I–I–I couldn't see."

"Then you should stay close," he heard Xanthe say, and the next moment he felt her hand take his own, their fingers entwining between one another. Takoda found himself grateful that the dust obscured his cheeks, which had begun shining brighter than any glowstone.

"Enough chatting," Meilin said, appearing in the thinning dust. "We have to stop the Many from destroying that bell tower." She crouched and swept her staff across the ground—tripping a flaming man on his way toward the city square.

"That tower is part of Kovo's plan to stop the Wyrm," Takoda explained to Xanthe. "If it falls, we're lost."

Xanthe stepped away from Takoda and raised a sort of horn made from a hollowed-out mushroom. She blew into one end, releasing a battle cry. "Protect the tower!" she cried. Soldiers streamed past her, running to the center of the city. They fought with determination and fury, cutting through the mob and forming a tight circle around the edge of the tower.

The Many were defenseless against the glowing crystalline blades of the Sadreans. Every cut seemed to scald the very flesh of those infected by the parasites— causing them to collapse to the ground, clutching their wounds as though they had been burned.

When the base of the tower had been secured, a small troop of white-haired slingmaidens positioned themselves on the remaining turrets, and they used the slings to launch glowstones on the Many below, driving them back into the shadows.

When the last of the Many had been vanquished, the Sadreans let out an enormous ululating cry that echoed in the caverns below. The sound was so strong that it made the roots overhead tremble, which in turn made Takoda tremble.

Conor, who had fought even more fiercely than the other Many, had finally been restrained by two burly Sadrean shieldwardens. They bound his arms behind his back and brought him to Meilin and Takoda. Briggan remained by their friend's side, while Jhi moved between the Sadreans, tending to their wounds as best she could.

"We only found the city just in time," Xanthe said, running to meet Takoda. "If those yellow flames had not appeared on the horizon, we might have gone off course and impaled our ships into the stalagmite reefs."

Takoda smiled, turning toward his spirit animal, who had positioned himself at the mouth of the tower—his great fists clutching the iron mallet, his small eyes trained on the Wyrm overhead. "The fire was Kovo's idea. He used it to drive back the Many." He shot Meilin a look. "Maybe you should thank him for saving our lives?" He still remembered the harsh things she had said about Kovo back in the lighthouse.

"I'll thank him when this is over," Meilin said darkly. She was still watching Conor, who seemed to have calmed down. The boy stared back at Meilin with empty, wrathful eyes. "Keeping this tower safe is only the beginning of this fight."

Xanthe stepped away from Takoda and knelt in front of Conor. "I'd assumed that you had abandoned him when he turned too far. That you carried him with you, even like this . . ." She looked down, and Takoda felt a pang of guilt. It was Xanthe who had been abandoned. And it had been his fault.

Conor gave a sharp snarl, lunging for Xanthe. The girl screamed, falling backward. The Sadrean shieldwardens kept him in place, but it was clear that something had happened to set him off. The possessed boy lurched up from the ground. All traces of the modest shepherd Takoda had first met in Nilo had vanished. Now he looked almost as inhuman as the Many. Conor snarled and hissed, staring upward with his dark eyes.

Briggan whined, backing away from his human partner.

"What's Conor doing?" Meilin said.

"Whatever he's doing, he's not alone." Xanthe pointed toward the shadowy city. "Look."

Takoda peered past the glowstone perimeter and saw that the surviving Many had emerged from the shadows, their long teeth flashing in the dim light as they all opened their mouths and made a sort of moaning sound. But they were no longer looking at the Sadrean army, or even the bell tower.

They were all staring upward, their long, bonelike fingers outstretched, swaying backward. The sounds of their moaning had a droning, almost hypnotic quality to it—like some sort of chant. Takoda couldn't help but think of the evening songs at his monastery.

A shivering *hsssssss* echoed through the darkness. Takoda looked up toward the egg, which was shaking and shuddering, trying to work its way free of the Evertree's roots. He heard a snapping sound as one of the thicker roots broke loose.

Rocks and dirt fell from the cavern ceiling, along with another huge snarl of root. It flopped to the floor, limp and dead—the silver glow already fading from it.

Takoda hadn't just heard the root breaking—he had *felt* it. The moment it happened, he gasped, staggering back. It was as though the very breath had been ripped from his chest. Meilin, too, seemed to have been similarly afflicted. She recovered and quickly placed Jhi into passive state—as if to fortify the spirit bond that had suddenly come under assault. Takoda tried to do the same, touching the place on his throat where Kovo dwelled in passive state, but the skin remained clammy and cold.

Kovo felt as distant from him as a stranger.

Another tendril of the Evertree's roots snapped, and this time the Wyrm's egg dropped several feet—its weight apparently too much for the young roots to bear. The egg thrashed and swung as whatever lived inside struggled to free itself.

The Many were now howling and shrieking, all reaching toward the Wyrm, all begging for it to free itself. Conor was howling with them, twisting his body and trying to get free of his restraints.

"Stay back!" Meilin cried, pulling Takoda and Xanthe clear of Conor's gnashing teeth. "Give him some space."

Kovo lumbered past her, right to Conor, and gave the boy a "tap" on the side of the head with the flat end of his mallet. The boy fell back to the ground—unconscious but otherwise unharmed. The Great Ape then turned toward Meilin and made a smug gesture with his hands: "Problem solved."

"Takoda!" Meilin snapped. "Get control of your spirit animal. Tell him if he touches my friend again, I'll make sure he lives to regret it."

"We've got bigger problems," Takoda said, his eyes fixed on the egg overhead. "The Wyrm is coming."

THE WYRM

Meilin stared at the Wyrm, unable to look away. More roots from the Evertree had snapped loose, and now the egg was hanging by a single thread. The egg itself was swinging and thrashing, as whatever was inside fought to free itself from the roots. Black ooze dripped from the large crack in the shell. Takoda could see dark and slimy tendrils moving between the fissures, writhing and twitching. Then the tendrils slid back, and he saw the red eye of the Wyrm, huge and searching.

Meilin heard a groaning sound as the last strand of the Evertree's roots snapped and the egg finally broke free. It fell down to the ground, landing with an earth-shaking shudder.

Rubble and smoke burst into the air. Meilin fell to one side, trying her best to protect Jhi from falling rubble. In the chaos, all she could hear were the snarls of the Many. And then above that, a new sound. A low, gurgling hiss that seemed to slither right up her spine and land in the back of her teeth.

As the dust cleared, Meilin rose and stared at the place where the egg had fallen. There was a dent in the stone floor from the impact. The shell had cracked open and now lay in several pieces. Black ooze seeped out from the spot, spreading across the ground in greedy little rivulets. And there, in the middle of it all, lay a roiling black knot of slick tendrils.

The arms—there must have been a dozen of them—slithered and flailed, pulling themselves apart like a knot untying itself. At the center of these was the Wyrm. The head—if you could call it a head—was somewhere in the middle of its enormous body. The thing blinked its red eyes—Meilin counted at least four—and then opened what must have been its mouth. It was a hideous, leechlike ring of razor-sharp teeth that seemed to flex and twist as it moved. The Wyrm let out a hoarse screech.

Meilin clutched her staff. "It's . . . like something from a nightmare."

She had been expecting to see a creature that looked like a lizard or salamander, or maybe even a snake, but the Wyrm did not appear so simple. Its movements were so fluid that it was difficult to grasp its full shape. Staring at it, Meilin was reminded of the way oil shifted and slid across the surface of water.

The appearance of the Wyrm seemed to have made an impact on the Many, who rushed closer to the glowstones— now unafraid of the searing light. They were all staring at the bell tower—at Meilin and her friends. The Wyrm was also facing them, its four eyes narrowed into hateful red slits. It screeched again, and the Many all charged through the perimeter—straight for the tower.

"Like I said," Meilin said, rotating her staff into a fighting position, "we've got a long way to go."

"Incoming!" Xanthe shouted, and then sounded the attack on her horn. "Brace for impact."

But trying to brace for this attack was like trying to stand up against the crashing tide. The Many hit them like a wave of claws and teeth—sweeping Sadrean fighters right off their feet as they rushed past. The Wyrm's army moved with a possessed fury—driven on by the shrieks of their master. Screams rang out as the Many grabbed hold of Sadrean soldiers and dragged them to the Wyrm as live offerings.

"Into the tower!" Meilin screamed, falling back with the others. She and Xanthe tried to close the iron doors, but they burst apart from the force of the frenzied mob. Meilin and Xanthe leaped back from the door and raced up the curved staircase, taking the steps two at a time. The Many were right behind them, hissing and clawing and snarling—climbing on top of one another to reach their prey.

Meilin brought Jhi into passive state to keep her safe. Briggan ran in front, attacking the few Many that had climbed in through the windows. Kovo had an unconscious Conor slung over one shoulder. Even with one hand, the Great Beast fought like a titan, grabbing the creatures and flinging them out open windows like rag dolls.

The entire tower shuddered and groaned as the horde began scaling the walls outside, tearing apart anything they could get ahold of. Meilin heard a scream as one of the slingmaidens was wrestled from her turret and thrown to the ground below—another offering for the Wyrm.

"Keep moving!" Meilin shouted. She felt like her heart would burst from running. She closed her eyes, forcing herself to climb even faster. They had to reach that bell before the tower came down on top of them.

At last she staggered onto the platform at the top of the tower. Briggan and Xanthe were close behind her. The huge iron bell hung in the middle of the room. Glowing moss covered the outside. This bell had been silent for thousands of years—waiting for this moment.

"Take care of the bell!" Meilin screamed to Kovo as she assumed a low position with her staff. "We'll hold the stairs."

Kovo dropped Conor and leaped clear over her head, landing behind her with a crash. He stomped toward the waiting bell, heaving the iron mallet over his head—

But then, he stopped.

The Great Beast gasped, stumbling backward as if he'd been pierced by some invisible blade. He lurched to one side. The iron mallet slid from his grasp and clunked to the floor.

"This is your chance, Kovo!" Meilin shouted over her shoulder. "What are you waiting for?!"

But the ape did not hear her. He had staggered away from the bell toward the window. Meilin saw that Xanthe had stopped fighting, too. She and Kovo were both staring outside.

Meilin grunted, kicking back a possessed Sadrean girl who was clawing at her boot. She ran to the window.

The moment she got there, she knew what had stopped Kovo and Xanthe. She saw the Wyrm writhing and shrieking at the foot of the tower—the ground around it was littered with the corpses of its prey. And clasped in one of its oozing tentacles was a small boy with dark hair, screaming for his very life.

"The Wyrm," Meilin whispered. "It's got Takoda."

SACRIFICE

I F IT HADN'T BEEN FOR TAKODA, XANTHE WOULD BE dead.

When Xanthe had first met Takoda in the caverns above Phos Astos, she thought him funny, if a little exotic. He was small, weak, and gentle. It was clear that he had no place among Meilin and the Greencloaks. When Xanthe learned that this quiet young monk was the human partner to the great Kovo she nearly laughed aloud.

But Xanthe soon realized that Takoda was nothing to laugh about. There was a strength to that boy, who could say more with a silent look than most people could with a thousand songs.

When Xanthe had been lost in the burned-out remnants of the Arachane Fields, alone and defenseless, it had been Takoda who kept her alive. She knew that she *had* to see him again—to make sure he was okay. She was afraid what might happen to him if she couldn't be there to help protect him from the Wyrm. And that fear had given her the strength to survive.

She had kept the sound of Takoda's voice in her mind as she wandered through the dark tunnels, without so much as a glowstone to find her way, until she finally stumbled into an intact Sadrean outpost—full of living, breathing, uninfected survivors.

In trying to save Takoda, Takoda had saved her.

Xanthe had continued thinking of him as she rallied those survivors and told them of the return of the Great Ape. Takoda was first in her thoughts as she led their fleet across the Sulfur Sea. And when the ships finally reached the ruined shore, and she saw Takoda's face amid the flames and rubble—the sight of him somehow opened up a part of her that she didn't even realize existed. It was as if she could see all of Erdas—the aboveground world she had only dreamed of—shining in his dark eyes.

And now, after all that struggle and pain, Takoda was about to die.

At first, Xanthe hadn't realized that Takoda had not made it into the tower with Meilin and the others. But when she heard his screams echoing up from the battle-field, she realized her error. She had abandoned him to die among the Many—to die as an offering to that oozing nightmare of tentacles and eyes and teeth that the elders called the Wyrm.

From the high window, she could now see the boy grasped in one of the Wyrm's arms. It was coiled around his body, crushing the life out of him. The Wyrm raised Takoda over its hideous mouth—its hundreds of drooling teeth twitching in anticipation of its next meal. Takoda dangled upside down, his face pale and bloodless, his gaze wide with terror and shock. His eyes looked upward, straight into hers.

For a moment all the sound seemed to vanish from the world. All Xanthe could hear was the dull throbbing of her own heartbeat.

"Takoda!" she shouted from the balcony. She slung her spear across her back and started to climb over the edge. "I'm coming!"

But before she could even put one leg over the railing, she was knocked to one side by Kovo. The Great Beast let out a terrifying roar and charged for the window. He dropped one knuckle down and leaped clean over the stone banister, sailing through the darkness and landing on the ground far below with a tremendous *crash!*

Kovo was on his feet again in a heartbeat, swinging his fists wildly as he bounded toward the Wyrm— sending the Many and the Sadreans alike scattering in all directions.

Xanthe had seen Kovo fight once before in Phos Astos, but that was nothing compared to what she witnessed now. The ape roared and lunged for the Wyrm, hurtling toward the creature with both fists drawn over his head.

The Wyrm, sensing the approach, flung Takoda to one side and raised its tentacles. Kovo's body hit it with the force of a cannonball, and the two of them spiraled backward across the ground, smashing clean through the wall of a building.

Xanthe's eyes scanned the teeming chaos below, searching for Takoda's body. But it was impossible to see from up here. She slung her spear over her shoulder. "We have to get Takoda," she said.

Meilin's hand grabbed her arm. "Don't you dare leave me up here!"

Xanthe turned around to see that the entire belfry had been overrun by the Many. Possessed Sadreans were swarming the bell and were trying to rip it free of its yoke. Briggan snarled and snapped, pulling them away with his jaws.

"That bell *is* the weapon," Meilin said. She swung her staff, knocking back an attacker who was trying to climb over the edge of the railing. "We have to ring it before the Many tear it to pieces."

"But Takoda's down there!" Xanthe yelled.

"Takoda can wait," Meilin said, kicking a hissing assailant square in the jaw. "This is war." Her voice was cold and without emotion, and Xanthe wondered just how much war this girl had seen in her lifetime. "Our mission is to stop that Wyrm before it can find a host. This tower won't stand much longer." She knelt down and wrapped her hands around the handle of the iron mallet. The thing was enormous—almost as big as she was. "Help me."

Xanthe tore herself from the window and grabbed the handle. She and Meilin both lifted at the same time, and the mallet's head rose from the ground. They carried it toward the bell—gaining speed as they moved. Acting as one, she and Meilin swung the mallet over their heads and—

WHAT LIES BENEATH

CLANGGGGG!!

The sound was almost deafening in Meilin's ears. The possessed Sadreans that had been clinging to the bell instantly fell away. The chime echoed and reverberated across the city, growing louder and louder.

Meilin staggered back with Xanthe, letting go of the mallet, which fell to the floor with a heavy thud. They had done it—the trap was sprung.

"What happens now?" Xanthe asked her.

Meilin shook her head. "I have no idea."

But it was clear that *something* was happening. The entire tower was trembling. Rubble sprinkled down on her as the platform—no, the entire structure—began to slowly rotate. Screams rang out from the ground below. Meilin ran to the window, Xanthe right behind her.

The ground was changing beneath them. The floor in the center of the city was drawing back like the folds of a paper fan to expose a dark chasm below. The Sadreans and the Many screamed, running to safety around the edges of the town.

"The ground is opening up around us," Meilin said.

That wasn't all the bell was doing. Meilin could feel something happening inside her—it felt like her stomach was turning inside out. She staggered to one side, suddenly unable to stand. She touched her tattoo to summon Jhi, but when the panda appeared at her side she, too, was showing the same symptoms. Meilin's vision blurred—like she was seeing two different things at once. It was almost like she could see herself outside of her own body.

Meilin and Jhi weren't the only ones. Briggan was whining over Conor's unconscious body, pawing at the boy.

"What's happening to you?" she heard Xanthe say.

"The snare," Meilin said through gritted teeth. "It's doing something to our spirit bonds." It felt like her whole body was dissolving with every breath.

She pulled herself to her knees and stared over the window railing. The tower was still turning slowly in the middle of the chasm, and it made her motion sick to stare at the ground below. She glimpsed Kovo staggering through the chaos. Red blood flowed from the Great Beast's body where the Wyrm's teeth had cut him. The ape stumbled and swayed, struggling to remain upright.

And then she saw the Wyrm. It was hissing, writhing in pain, its movements jerky and uncontrolled. The infected Sadreans around the Wyrm had stopped moving completely, as if the breath had just gone out of them. Whatever was happening to Meilin and Jhi looked like it was also happening to the Wyrm and its minions—only on a much bigger scale. "It's working!" Meilin cried, gripping the bannister. "The Wyrm's guard is down. . . . This is our chance . . . to kill it. . . ."

But then, with a sharp jolt, the tower stopped moving. Meilin lurched to one side, nearly falling to the floor. She heard a groaning sound as the gears deep within the tower walls strained against something that was blocking their motion. It shuddered and then stopped altogether. "No!" Meilin said, scrambling to her feet. "Keep going!" She kicked the iron bell, trying to start the mechanism, but it was useless.

The snare had stopped.

Already Meilin's head felt clearer—whatever had been happening between her and Jhi had halted along with the tower. She clenched her teeth and struggled to stay upright. She looked to the battlefield and saw that the Wyrm had also recovered. It released a furious shriek, and the Many around it seemed to snap back to attention.

Meilin watched as the creature slithered toward the edges of the hole that had half opened up before it—the doors halted along with the tower. It reached a quivering tentacle out into the void. The tentacle flicked like the tongue of a serpent tasting the air. With a screech that seemed to echo as much in Meilin's own mind as it did across the crumbling city, the Wyrm slithered forward and melted into the darkness.

A few of the Many leaped into the hole after their master. Their cries echoed for several seconds as their bodies plummeted down. The rest of the Many broke formation and scurried away from the light of the flames and Sadrean blades—disappearing into the darkness of the outlying tunnels.

"Is it over?" Xanthe whispered beside her.

Meilin shook her head, her eyes fixed on the bottomless hole. It seemed to plunge down straight through the heart of Erdas. "I don't think so." She ran her hand through Jhi's fur, taking comfort in the warmth of her spirit animal—in the strength of the bond they shared.

Meilin heard Briggan yip behind her. The wolf was bleeding badly from his side where the Many had attacked him. Conor lay unconscious beside him, bleeding, pale, but still alive. Briggan pointed his muzzle toward the stairs and Meilin and Xanthe followed him out of the tower.

Meilin and the others stepped outside to find Kovo at the far edge of the chasm, clutching Takoda in his enormous arms like one might hold an infant.

Jhi ambled to the boy, tending to an ugly gash in his chest—the place where the Wyrm's tentacle had pierced through him.

"Takoda!" Xanthe cried, rushing to his side. The girl took Takoda's hand in her own. The boy's face was gray. He had clearly lost a lot of blood.

"Is he . . . ?" Meilin said, unable to form the question.

"He's alive," Xanthe said, her voice shaking. "Kovo saved his life."

Meilin sighed, swallowing down her worst fears. She was glad, but also heartbroken. All this destruction, and for what? They had failed in their mission. "We may be alive, but so is the Wyrm," she said. "And I have a feeling it's headed straight for Zerif." She tried not to think of Rollan and Abeke having to face that creature. She met Kovo's eyes. "Still. Thank you. Leaping out from the tower to save Takoda . . . I didn't think you had it in you."

The gorilla huffed, blinking.

"The snare was working, just like you said it would," Meilin said. "But then it stopped. What happened?"

Kovo shook his head: *I don't know.* He made several gestures with his hand. Before Meilin could explain that she didn't understand his signs, Takoda stirred, turning toward her. "Kovo says . . . the snare is jammed." He swallowed. "Something must have stopped it from turning . . . something on the other side."

"So just like that, it's over?" Meilin said. She could feel her eyes welling up. "All this death. All this pain. Just so we could lose by something *getting jammed*?"

The Great Beast made a series of angry gestures—he looked as frustrated as she did about the failure of the snare. "All is not lost," Takoda said, struggling to translate. "There is a second bell, at the place where your friends are. If they can ring it, there may be a chance. . . ."

"Do they know about the bell?" Meilin said, stepping closer. "Do the others know how the snare works?"

Kovo lowered his hand, shaking his head.

"I don't know," Takoda said.

Meilin released a long breath, exchanging a look with Xanthe. "Well then . . . let's hope they figure it out fast . . . while there's still an Erdas to save."

TO ARMS

BEING A LEADER IS OFTEN DIFFICULT. IT REQUIRES THAT you continually put the needs of others before your own desires.

When Shane was the king of Stetriol, his uncle Gar had once told him he should put his will first—rule with an iron fist. Even then—as he made some of the worst mistakes ever witnessed by the long history of Erdas—Shane had known better. It wasn't a fist that had won him the Greencloaks' talismans. Sacrifices had.

Sacrifices he now regretted.

Shane stood crouched in the icy chamber where, a moment before, he, Abeke, and Rollan had been communing with the Great Beast Kovo. The same Great Beast who had once manipulated him into collecting the talismans and conquering the world.

"Zerif's found us?" he said, clutching Niri's arm. "Are you sure?"

The girl, whose eyes had returned to a sea green color, nodded. "He's got a fleet of ships with him and he's heading this way." Niri's spirit animal, Mulop, had already withdrawn from the chamber and was now swimming in the cold open waters. She tilted her head to one side, as though hearing a voice. "They'll be here by nightfall."

"So soon!" Rollan muttered. "And here I was hoping we'd have a snowball fight!"

Shane stood and shot him an icy glare. "This is no time for jokes," he said as he marched toward the main tunnel, his hand resting on the hilt of his saber.

"I disagree," Rollan said, following after him. "This is the *perfect* time for jokes—then at least we can die with smiles on our faces!"

"Wouldn't that require actually being funny?" Shane said, raising an eyebrow. He was gratified to see Abeke purse her lips in an attempt not to laugh at her friend. Shane turned toward the tunnel. "We have to get aboveground."

"Wait!" Niri called after him. She was pulling herself upright at the edge of the water with her thin arms. By her strained expression, it was clear that the maneuver took all her strength. "There's something . . . I can still hear them talking in Sadre." She swallowed. "Mulop is too weak to speak with them, but he can still hear what they're saying to Kovo. . . ."

"You can hear Meilin?" Rollan said, stepping toward her. "Is she talking about me?" He swallowed. "Or, um, Abeke? Any of us really? Forget I asked."

Niri shook her head, screwing up her face. "They're arguing about something. It has to do with the snare and the Wyrm and . . ." She winced and then sighed. "It's hard to follow."

"Keep trying," Shane said, moving into the tunnel. "In the meantime, we need to prepare for war."

"Um, maybe we should listen to her?" Rollan said, hanging back.

"Your girlfriend can wait!" Shane shouted, drawing his sword. "I have fifty Redcloaks up there who are depending on me to lead them. Not to mention the other Great Beast summoners. Zerif is coming, and we need every hand we can get. That includes you. Now let's move."

Shane knew it was a mistake to give someone like Rollan direct orders, but that didn't seem to be the problem at the moment. Rollan was concerned with something else that he had heard.

"G-g-girlfriend?" he stammered, his cheeks turning crimson. "Who said anything about that?"

Shane rolled his eyes and swept up the tunnel. Abeke followed close behind him, her bow drawn. "You really think we can fend off Zerif's army?" she said. "They're as fast as they are deadly. We both saw him take down the greatest fortress in Nilo in a matter of hours."

"We're not in Zourtzi anymore," Shane said. "And Faisel was unprepared. The Hellans took more than a few precautions when building this place. We'll be ready for them." He slowed, fixing his eyes on her. "I promise."

Abeke sighed, not meeting his gaze. "I've heard that before."

Shane nodded, feeling the sting of her words. "You're right," he said, realizing that words—no matter how sincere—would never win her trust. He wondered how many times he would have to save her life before she began to believe that he was truly changed.

As many times as it takes, he silently promised himself.

The trip aboveground seemed to last forever. Shane's Redcloaks hadn't had a chance to map all the twisting tunnels in the base of the mountain, and it was difficult to navigate without Yumaris at his side. Soon, however, he found himself at an open ledge in the main chamber of the ruins, where the volcano's cauldron had been blocked off with stone.

If Kovo was to be believed, beneath that stone floor was a tunnel that went straight to the Evertree. And somehow these two sets of ruins contained enough power to stop the Wyrm. If only they knew how.

The bleating trumpet of a conch shell sounded in the camp, signaling that the watchmen had spotted ships approaching.

Already Shane could hear the footsteps of his fellow Redcloaks as they rushed up and down the footpaths. The open pathways wound inside the volcano like a spool of thread.

His Redcloaks were preparing for battle. They had known this day was coming, and they were ready.

Stead met Shane halfway down the lower stairs. Shadow and Jolt were behind him. "How close are they?" Shane said, joining Stead's side. "What are their numbers?"

Stead shook his head. "We're not sure, King. Our lookouts spotted ships on the horizon, but we can't see more than that."

"I can tell you," Rollan said, following a few feet behind. He put a hand to his temple. "Essix was flying out in that direction. I'll take a peek."

Rollan closed his eyes and tilted his head upward. "She's flying better now," he said. "I think she's gotten over the pull of the poles enough to fly straight." He drew in a sharp breath and his skin turned a slight greenish. "Sorry . . . a little motion sick."

"Do you see Zerif's ship?" Abeke said, taking Rollan's hand.

Rollan nodded. "I do. Along with one . . . two . . . three . . . four . . . five others."

"Half a dozen ships?" Stead said, looking to Shane. "That's an entire fleet."

"Whatever it is, we'll be waiting for them," Shane said, refusing to let his own concern cloud his face. "Good work, Rollan," he said. "Now tell Essix to get back here before she's spotted by Zerif's men."

He knew from experience that Zerif and his army of enslaved Greencloaks wouldn't hesitate to send their own flying spirit animals after the falcon.

"Oh, they saw her, all right," Rollan said, opening his eyes. "She swooped over the deck and left a little, er, *present* for Zerif." He broke into a devilish grin.

Shane shook his head. "I know you only saw them for a brief moment, but did you get a count of how many crewmen Zerif has?"

Rollan's smile faltered. "Maybe a hundred Greencloaks—and that was just above deck."

Shane nodded gravely. "There's probably another hundred below. That means we're outnumbered almost four to one." He became aware of Abeke watching him.

"You don't seem worried about those odds," she said.

Shane gave her a smile that he could only hope looked herolike. "We've got a *few* tricks up our sleeves." He turned to Stead and the other Redcloaks. "Get to your stations. Don't act until I give the signal."

Stead and the others saluted and ran off in different directions. He watched as Jolt leaped from rock to rock, until he had reached a platform with a window that looked out over the water. Already the Redcloaks had assembled javelins made of ice for throwing at the landing party.

"I was kidding when I said I wanted a snow fight," Rollan said. "You really think icicles will stop Zerif's army?"

"They don't have to. All we need to do is slow down Zerif's forces and cut them off with the lava flows." So saying, he led them to a small platform cut into the side of the rock that overlooked the sea. Along one wall was an iron contraption made from ancient gears and levers that went straight down through the heart of the mountain. He didn't know how they all worked, and the main set of gears had remained stubbornly in place even when his best tinkerer, a girl named Talon, had tried to release them. He suspected those ancient gears were somehow connected to the Sadrean city on the other side of the world.

"What do you want us to do?" Abeke said.

Shane nodded, pulling a lever in the wall. A small door opened and a stream of molten lava oozed out, running down a small channel that was dug into the floor. "Zerif's still looking for the last of the Great

Beasts—the smart thing would be for us to keep Rollan, Kirat, and Tasha out of the fight."

"Yeah, but you know that's not going to happen," Rollan said, his hand on his dagger. "Besides, this is the end of the line. Either we fend off Zerif, or it's over for good."

"Much as it pains me to say it, I think you've got a point," Shane said, pulling another lever to release more lava down another channel. "Especially now that we know his numbers. There's a lava gate on the eastern end of the volcano that needs soldiers. One of my best Redcloaks, Howl, is already there, but he might need help to operate the mechanism."

"We'll do our best," Abeke said.

"Good," Shane said, nodding. "Warn Tasha and Kirat to be careful with their spirit animals—that's why Zerif is here in the first place. They should keep Ninani and Cabaro passive, if possible. Only summon them if it's a true emergency."

"Speaking of Great Beasts," Rollan said. "Right as we were leaving, Niri was trying to tell us something about Meilin and Takoda. They were saying something to Kovo—don't you think one of us should check on her?"

"There isn't time," Shane snapped. Why did this kid have to question his every order? He was trying to keep them safe. "Niri is safe for now belowground. We'll have to worry about Kovo and the Wyrm once we've taken care of Zerif. For now, I need you to watch after the others."

"We're about to dive into war and you want us babysitting," Rollan said. "You sure this isn't just a way to keep us out of your hair?"

Shane couldn't resist a small grin. "Can't it be both?" He turned on his heel and rushed into the tunnels, his red cloak flapping behind him.

KIRAT

ROLLAN AND ABEKE WERE LEFT TO FIND THEIR OWN way to the camp. Redcloaks ran all around them, shouting commands—some of them sounding more animal than human when they spoke. As soon as Rollan set foot outside of the warmth of the volcano, he was again struck by just how cold this place was. Icy wind swept past him, going straight through his threadbare cloak.

"You'd think the Hellans could have picked a warmer spot," he said, rubbing his arms.

"They didn't have a choice," Abeke said, trudging forward through the snow. "They needed to build along the axis of Erdas. I'm guessing that the snare somehow manipulates the magnetic forces swirling around this point—the same forces that confuse compass needles and make it difficult for Essix to fly."

Rollan wasn't sure how magnetic forces could stop the Wyrm, but he chose not to argue the point. It was clear from the conversation with Kovo that there was more to these ruins than he could understand. Essix, for her part, seemed glad to see Rollan out in the open, and she allowed herself to be put into passive state—if for no other reason than to warm up before another flight.

The outer camp of the island was made up of a series of deep, icy trenches that stretched in every direction. Rollan recalled what Shane had said about the lava flues, and he wondered if these trenches were actually part of the mountain's defenses.

They soon found their way to the shelter where the bereft had been staying. The room was empty but for Tasha, however, whose face and eyes were red. Rollan realized that she had been crying. Ninani the Swan sat next to her, trying to comfort her by rubbing her head against Tasha's hand.

"What's going on?" Abeke asked. "Where are the others?"

"They heard the conch shell and shouts of alarm." Tasha shook her head. "I tried to tell them they had to stay, but . . . but *he* wouldn't listen." She stomped the snowy ground.

"Let me guess," Rollan said, folding his arms. "Kirat?"

"We need them," Abeke said. "Where did they go?"

Tasha and Ninani led them to the icy port where the *Expiator* was moored. Kirat and the other children were standing at the bottom of the gangplank, caught in an argument with Devin Trunswick—or Worthy or Wiggly—whatever he was calling himself.

"I *command* you to step aside!" Kirat shouted, one hand on the hilt of his rapier. "We are commandeering this vessel!"

The Redcloak folded his arms across his chest, laughing. "You'll have to do better than that." Rollan had to admit: Devin's new catlike eyes truly complemented his smug, disinterested demeanor.

"Come on, Devin!" whined one of the other children, a curly-haired boy Rollan only now recognized as *Dawson* Trunswick. "Let us through."

"No way, little brother," said the Redcloak. "I'm not moving unless King says so. Besides, we need these cannons to fend off the incoming ships."

"Wait," Rollan said, stepping in front of Kirat. "You're trying to take Shane's ship?"

"It's not *Shane's* ship," Kirat snapped. "It belongs to Cordalles's family." He nodded to one of the children huddled around him. "She loaned it to the Redcloaks, and now she wants it back."

"And I wonder who gave her that idea?" Rollan muttered.

"Enough," Abeke said, putting herself between the two boys. "Zerif's found us. His ships will be here before sundown."

Kirat rolled his eyes. "Obviously. The only question is whether or not you two are stupid enough to stick around and die with the rest of those red-cloaked freaks." He gestured to the other children, who were all huddled around him. "Do what you want, but *we're* getting out of here."

"You cowardly little snot!" Tasha said, pushing toward him. "Rollan and Abeke risked their lives to rescue you from Zerif!"

"They brought a marauding army to my father's doorstep!" Kirat shouted, his voice cracking with real emotion. "My life was perfect before they showed up! And make no mistake, they care nothing for me or you. They only care about our precious spirit animals."

Rollan peered around, looking for Cabaro. "Where is that big cat anyway?"

Kirat glared at him superciliously. "He's in passive state, of course." He pulled back his collar to reveal a lion-shaped tattoo on the back of his neck. "He finally accepted who his master is." Even though Kirat's fingers had touched the tattoo, Cabaro had still not appeared.

"Let me guess, *master*," Rollan said, a grin playing at the edge of his mouth. "He went passive and now he won't come back?"

Kirat's dark cheeks turned darker. "I don't need a spirit animal anyway—all he did was lie around and take up space."

"Can we save the bickering for *after* the battle?" Abeke said. "The Redcloaks need help—from all of us. And they need this ship's cannons to defend the shore. Zerif has eight Great Beasts at his command and a fleet of ships filled with Greencloaks. Do you really think you can evade that?"

"We don't have to," Kirat said, sniffing. "If Zerif wants Great Beasts, he can have mine. I'll turn Cabaro over myself in exchange for my life."

"You'd have to summon him first," Rollan muttered.

Abeke shot him a glare that seemed to say that he wasn't helping things. "Turning over the Great Beasts is not an option," she said flatly.

"That's easy for you to say!" said an Ardu girl named Anuqi. "You still have your spirit animals—you have something worth fighting for. Some of us have lost our families, our homes, everything. Why is it always *fight* with you Greencloaks?"

Rollan looked at Abeke, knowing how the girl's words must have stung. "Actually, I *don't* have a spirit animal," Abeke said in a quiet voice. "Zerif took control of Uraza when we were in Nilo." She lowered her head.

Rollan put a hand on Abeke's shoulder, a pathetic attempt at consolation. "You'll always be a Greencloak," he said.

"Save your sob stories for someone who cares," Kirat said, planting his hands on his hips. "We're done being pawns in your little Greencloak spat." The other children muttered in agreement.

"This isn't a *spat!*" Rollan shouted, feeling like he might very well explode on the spot. "We're *trying* to save the world!"

He felt a hand on his arm. It was Abeke. "Yelling isn't going to make them fight," she said gently. She pulled Rollan back from the group, speaking in a low voice. "Look at them. They're scared. Most of them have already lost their spirit animals. That's a pain greater than you could ever understand." And here her face flickered with the pain of her own loss—of her own Uraza ripped from her. "They don't need threats. They need a reason to keep on living. They need to be inspired."

Rollan rolled his eyes. "Inspiration really isn't my style." He desperately wished that Meilin were there—she would certainly know how to rally their spirits.

Abeke nodded, dropping her voice even lower. "We already have a born leader in our midst." She nodded to

Kirat, who had resumed his argument with Devin on the gangplank.

"Kirat?" Rollan said. "You've got to be kidding."

Abeke shrugged. "Perhaps we've done him an injustice by treating him like a helpless child. He was not raised to take orders, he was raised to lead. Don't forget, Tarik's blood runs in his veins."

The mention of Tarik's name put a lump in Rollan's throat. Their old Greencloak mentor had been the only adult who had ever really believed in Rollan. He had trusted Rollan when everyone had lost faith in him. And Rollan knew that Tarik would want him to show that same faith in his nephew. "Ugh," he muttered. "I hate it when you're right."

Abeke nodded to him and together they stepped past the other Great Beast summoners, approaching Kirat. The boy had been scratching Cabaro's mark on his neck with no success at drawing forth the Great Lion. "We owe you an apology," she said.

"Keep your apologies," Kirat said, lowering his hand. "I'd rather keep my life."

Abeke nudged Rollan, and he realized that she was expecting him to do the talking.

Rollan was good at begging, at lying, at swindling for food, but not *this*. He took a breath, trying to think about what he could say to make Kirat understand. He tried to imagine how Kirat felt in this moment, having fled from the destruction of his home to find himself in this desolate place.

"It's okay to be scared," Rollan said slowly. "But it's not okay to run from your duty. You agreed to protect these children, and they're depending on you. Your father fought before giving up Zourtzi. Do you really think he would run in this situation?"

The mention of Kirat's father was clearly a sore spot, and the boy's face softened slightly.

"The Redcloaks need this ship, not to mention the extra hands," Abeke added. "These others won't listen to us—we're wearing the same cloaks as the army that's coming this way. But they will listen to you. You're a trained fighter, and you've spent a lifetime watching your father build and protect the greatest fortress in all of Nilo by inspiring thousands of subjects. We need you to lead."

Rollan reached into his pack and removed a small amulet with an iron chain. "This belonged to your uncle, Tarik." He held out the chain for Kirat to see. "The man you were named after. He died trying to protect the world from Zerif. And now it's your turn to join the fight." He ran his thumb over the cracked green stone. "Your mother gave it to me. She told me I should save it for when you were ready to follow in his footsteps. It was her last wish."

Kirat's face softened even more. "She . . . my mother told you that?"

Rollan nodded. "She did. The only question now is: Are you ready?"

Kirat reached out a hand, which Rollan couldn't help but notice was shaking. The boy took the amulet and stared at it in the cold afternoon light. He held it for what felt like an eternity. Then he dipped his head and placed the chain around his neck. It was not an expensive amulet—Kirat's silken socks were probably worth more than the common gemstone—but when the boy raised his face again, he looked more richly garbed than any prince Rollan had ever seen.

Kirat turned away from them and faced the other children, who were huddled at the bottom of the gangplank, waiting for him to speak.

"Are we going?" asked Cordalles. "We're running out of time."

"There's no time." Kirat took a deep breath and turned toward them. "I did you a disservice by leading you to this port—by letting you think there was a way out of danger. I claimed that it was the smart thing to do. But it wasn't intellect that motivated me. It was cowardice."

"Better to live a coward than die a hero," said Dawson.

"You're probably right," Kirat said, shrugging. "I've never been too impressed by courage. I remember my tutors and scrollmavens talking fondly about courageous heroes falling in battle. Hearing those songs and ballads, I always thought that it was a flimsy reward for losing one's life." A few of the children chuckled at this nervously. "But really," Kirat continued, "all my scorn for courage was an attempt to cover up my fear. My whole life has been dominated by fear. My father was the most powerful merchant lord in all Nilo, second only to the high chieftain. Some would have called him a tyrant. I was terrified of him. But all his soldiers and battlements and might were nothing in the face of Zerif's army." He closed his eyes, taking a deep breath.

"Not exactly the rousing speech we were hoping for," Rollan muttered.

"Shh," Abeke whispered. "At least they're listening."

Rollan looked at the other children and saw that Abeke was right. The children were hanging on to Kirat's every word, some of them even nodding. "I'm done being afraid," the young lord continued. "I've already lost everything. My family, my wealth, my home. You have all lost even more than that—having your spirit animals ripped from you. Which means you have nothing to fear. How can we possibly fear a thing like death, when we've nothing to live for?" The boy stood before them, his uncle's amulet glinting against the afternoon sun. "Truly, it is Zerif who should fear *us*."

He paced in front of them, raising his voice, speaking more quickly. "We are not ordinary children. We didn't just summon spirit animals. We are the first in the history of Erdas to summon *Great Beasts*." He pointed to different children as he spoke. "Rumfuss the Boar . . . Suka the Polar Bear . . . Halawir the Eagle . . . Arax the Ram . . . Tellun the Elk . . . Dinesh the Elephant."

"But Dinesh is gone," said a Zhongese girl. "So are the rest of the Beasts." She had tears standing in her dark eyes.

Kirat nodded. "Dinesh may be gone, but you remain, Kaiina. And you have his resilience within you." He spread his arms wide. "The same is true for all of us. Our beasts didn't just come to human partners at random. They came to *us* . . . because each of us has something inside ourselves that reflects the nature of our Great Beasts. The wisdom of the elk, the courage of the eagle, the determination of the ram, the cunning of the boar, the strength of the polar bear." His eyes flicked to Tasha and Ninani. "The grace of the swan."

Rollan looked at Tasha and the other children. They were all watching Kirat with intense expressions. A few of them looked like they were about to cry. Rollan had to admit that Kirat had a way with words.

Kirat paced in front of them, standing tall. "But this is not a time for mourning. This is a time for action. The same Great Beasts that came to each of us have now been captured by a force more evil than any Erdas has ever faced. They need our help." He drew his gilded rapier from its sheath, raising it over his head. "Would we really turn our backs on them? Or will we FIGHT?!"

"We fight!" the children cried. There was a flash and the next moment Cabaro stood beside Kirat. The lion raised his head and released a tremendous roar that rocked the boat and shook the water.

The other children stared at the beast in awe. Rollan stared, too. It seemed the great Cabaro had suddenly decided to lend his support to his human partner. And Rollan thought he understood why. This was a whole new Kirat.

THE BATTLE BEGINS

W HILE ABEKE AND KIRAT LED THE NEWLY ENERGIZED children into the caverns, Rollan remained outside to let Essix stretch her wings and fly a few laps around the mountain. He watched her soaring through the cold air and wondered what it would feel like to be so high above the world. He could, of course, share her vision and see it, but that wasn't the same.

"You make sure to stay safe for what's coming," he said to the falcon as she landed again on his arm. Win or lose, he didn't want to end up like the other Great Beast summoners. Like Abeke.

By the time Rollan caught up with them in the caverns, he found them all paired off in sparring formation, each clutching swords. Kirat stood in front with Tasha, who had her staff and was preparing to charge.

"Keep your knees bent," Kirat said instructively. "Don't watch your opponent's eyes or even their hands— the feet can tell you everything you need to know. Wait for them to make the first move, and when they are transferring weight between feet"—he swung the dull end of his rapier under Tasha's leg as she charged—"you draw your weapon in the opposite direction." Tasha flipped backward, landing hard on her back. "Let their movement work against them."

Several of the children managed to apply this technique with similar success. Rollan clapped, stepping into the room. "Not bad," he said. "Seems you were paying attention to my lessons on the *Expiator.*"

"Only as an example of what *not* to do," Kirat said, stiffening. "I enjoyed seven years of training under the best duelists in all of Nilo. It's time I put that knowledge to use."

Rollan couldn't help but smile. It seemed that even the new-and-improved Kirat could still talk back. He turned to Abeke, who was at the far wall conferring with Howl, his face covered with a white coyote mask.

"What's going on over here?" he said.

"We're stuck." Howl shook his head, his ears twitching slightly behind the mask. "We need to raise this lava gate, but it's encased in ice." He pulled against a lever that refused to budge. "We could melt it with torches, but that could take an hour."

"Allow me," Kirat said, joining them. He nodded to Cabaro, who was crouched behind him. The lion rose to his feet and moved to the lever. With one swipe of his mighty claw, the ice shattered, releasing the gate's lever.

"Problem solved," Abeke said.

Howl pulled the lever, which now moved easily. There was a ratcheting sound inside the cavern wall, and then a stone gate opened near Rollan's feet. Steaming lava slid from the hole and ran down a groove in the cavern floor, filling up a sort of cauldron at the edge of the window. "So how does this work?" Rollan said.

Howl pointed at the basin of bubbling lava. "This fills up to create pressure. Like a water tank. And when we pull the main winch"—he hiked his furry thumb at a huge handle—"then the basin will drain into those trenches around the perimeter."

"A lava moat," Rollan said. "Not bad."

"It could be better," Kirat said. He didn't sound arrogant, just matter-of-fact. "What if we used archers to drive the incoming forces to that ice shelf near the edge of the island? Then when the lava sweeps through, it will drop them into the freezing sea."

Rollan, Abeke, and Howl all looked at Kirat, who blushed. "It's . . . just an idea."

"No, it's a great idea," Howl said.

Rollan had to agree. He may have enjoyed more experience in hand-to-hand combat, but he knew nothing about strategy. "There's one problem," he said. "Those are still Greencloaks out there—possessed or not. They're our friends. We're not going to kill them."

"Our *friends*?" Kirat turned toward him, eyes flashing. "Tell that to everyone in this room who's had their family killed." The boy shook his head, taking a deep breath. Rollan could actually see him forcing back his own emotions. "I know this is hard for you, Rollan. But this is war. And if we don't stop them, a lot more people will die."

"He's right," Abeke said. "We can't let our feelings about the Greencloaks get in the way of stopping Zerif."

Rollan looked at Abeke, shocked to hear such a thing coming from her. Then again, she was a hunter. She always had more of a killer instinct than he did. "Fine," he said, sighing. "But let's at least try to keep the casualties to a minimum."

"I'll alert Shane to prepare the archers," Abeke said, stepping back.

Rollan still didn't feel completely comfortable with Shane. And he knew that Abeke's feelings were even more complicated.

"You fighting with Shane . . ." he said carefully. "Are you sure that's a good idea?"

"He'll need archers," she said firmly, "and I'm the best shot he's got."

Howl pulled up his mask and offered a toothy grin. "Don't let Talon hear you say that. She's a master with a crossbow."

The debate was cut off by the sound of a conch shell from one of the lookouts. Rollan and the others all rushed to the window and peered out over the frozen sea.

Zerif's fleet was fast approaching: six ships surrounded by a swirling cloud of white fog. The cloud lifted up from the boats and moved closer to them—growing larger and larger.

"What is that stuff?" Rollan said. "It's too cold for fog."

Howl narrowed his lupine eyes. "That's not fog." He ran to the tunnel and cupped both hands around his mouth. "INCOMING!" he hollered. "Everyone! Back from the windows!"

The next minute a snowy tern darted through the window and plunged its beak straight into Tasha's leg.

She screamed, and before Rollan or anyone else could react, Cabaro pounced on the bird and snatched it in his mighty jaws. He snapped the bird's neck and flung it to the ground. The tern lay dead and twitching, its head marked with the swirl of Zerif's parasite.

Rollan looked out the window and saw that the cloud was really thousands of birds—all flying toward them at deadly speed. He ducked to one side as three more snowy terns darted into the window, each one hurtling toward a different target. There were screams all through the camp as birds swept into the mountain, attacking Redcloaks. They were not hard to beat away, but there were so many of them that it was nearly impossible to see.

"Defensive position!" Kirat called, and they all raced to the middle of the room, backs together.

The air shuddered as he heard cannon fire from the *Expiator*. Rollan and Essix fought against two birds that were swarming around Abeke. The war had begun.

Essix screeched, grabbing a possessed tern in her razor claws. "Go!" Rollan cried, slicing his dagger through the other bird's extended wing. Abeke locked eyes with Rollan for one last moment, and then she was gone.

FLAMES AND FROST

ABEKE RACED THROUGH THE TUNNELS TO THE ARCHERS' keep along the high rim of the volcano. She didn't want to admit it, but she was glad to be away from the other Great Beast summoners—she had been afraid that Howl would insist that she belonged with them. Zerif's terns squawked and slashed through the caverns. The Redcloaks had drawn their arms and were swiping at the birds, chasing them through the maze of tunnels.

"The birds are a distraction!" Abeke yelled. "Everyone stay at your posts!"

Abeke followed the winding path that moved up the inside of the volcano. The path led her through an archway that was nearly as high as the icy tower. She ran through the arch to find a narrow cavern with a series of slat windows cut into the rock—the archers' keep. Shane was there with a handful of other Redcloaks. Yumaris was with him, too, huddled in the corner, fending off an attacking bird that had found its way through the slats. Abeke drew her own bow, quickly nocked an arrow, and cut through the bird—killing it in one shot.

"Oh, bless you, hollow-girl," the old woman said. "That early birdie was trying to get the worm."

"Don't mention it," Abeke gasped. Steam rose from her mouth as she struggled to catch her breath. Icy wind whistled through the windows, covering the floor of the cavern with a thin layer of snow. Apparently the Hellans' lava channels couldn't go this high.

"What are *you* doing here?" asked the birdlike girl named Talon. She was loading a bolt into her crossbow. "Shouldn't you be babysitting the others?" She took aim and shot her bolt straight through the heart of an approaching tern, which veered off course and slammed into the opposite wall.

"Change of plans," Abeke said, lowering her bow. "We need to save our arrows for the landing party. We'll drive them to the far trench by the water and then release the lava gates."

"Who died and put you in charge?" Talon said, her sharp eyes darting between Abeke and the window.

"No," Shane said, stepping to Abeke's side. "It's a good plan." He turned to the row of archers. "Hold fire. Let's wait out this first wave until Zerif lands."

Another possessed bird swept through the window.

"What's the point of waiting if we've been pecked to pieces by the time Zerif gets here?!" shouted a boy with a bear mask. He snarled, swatting at the possessed bird, which was trying to claw out his eyes.

Shane drew his sword and cut toward the bird, sending it wheeling out of the tower. "We'll have to find some other way to take the birds out." He turned back toward Talon. "Tell Stead to release the gate on balcony number six!"

Talon ran to the archway and shouted the command into the tunnel. The order echoed down the mountain until it reached Stead's ears. A moment later, a vent of simmering lava spilled out from the side of the rock, directly onto a pile of loosely packed snow at the base of the mountain. The snow hissed and melted to create a huge cloud of billowing vapor. The cloud was enough to blind the incoming birds, which suddenly were unable to navigate. Pained squawks rang out as the soaring flock missed their targets and instead crashed against the outside wall of the mountain.

"Nice work," Abeke said, shivering.

Shane's astonished smile at this meager praise sent a tremor of guilt through Abeke's chest. He looked like she'd just kissed him on the cheek.

Catching himself, the leader of the Redcloaks coughed, pursing his lips into a thin line. "The birds were just a distraction," he said brusquely. "The real fight is still to come."

The ground shook as two mortar shells from the incoming fleet struck the side of the mountain—Zerif's fleet was now in firing range. There was the sound of an explosion near the port, and Abeke watched as the *Expiator* burst into splinters and sank into the cold water.

"There goes our ride home," Abeke said as the ship's mast slid below the surface. She stared at the approaching fleet, half shrouded in smoke from the cannon fire, searching for a sight of Zerif's dark tunic.

"Ready arrows!" Shane called. "Wait for my mark." He and the other Redcloaks positioned themselves at the windows. "There's a cache of arrows along the back wall," he said to Abeke.

"Thanks, but I brought my own." Abeke drew back her green cloak and removed a single arrow from her full quiver. The black point glinted in the light of the setting sun—it was sharpened obsidian. She had spent most of her voyage honing them to razor points—sharp enough to cut through any armor or shield Zerif might use. She nocked it into the string of her bow, steadying her aim.

"Obsidian points," Shane said, eyeing her full quiver. "How many of those are for Zerif?"

Abeke tightened her grip on the end of the nocked arrow. "As many as it takes."

"I'd hate to have you as an enemy," he said weakly. "Again."

Abeke looked at him, unable to tell if this was a joke. It was harder to read his expressions now—the reptilian glint in his eyes made him appear less human.

"I'm not going to shoot you, if that's what you're asking," she said, turning back to the window. She had thought about it, of course. But whatever anger she felt toward Shane was tempered by her memory of their time together among the Conquerors.

Once, Shane had been a guide and friend to her. Maybe the first true friend she ever had. He had been the one who taught Abeke that she could find family wherever she was and encouraged her to find it in Uraza.

There was another rumbling sound—much louder than the mortar shots. Abeke placed her hand on the ledge to keep herself from falling. She could feel the entire mountain shaking from the vibrations. "Sounds like they found a bigger cannon," she said.

"Not a cannon, hollow-girl," Yumaris said, shaking her head. She touched the ground, which was still shaking. "Something much bigger. Something deep below . . ."

The old woman gestured for them to come to the archway and look inside the mountain. Abeke joined her. The icy tower in the middle of the volcano was slowly rotating, dropping huge chunks of ice onto the floor. She feared the ice might crush the Redcloaks, but when she looked farther down, she saw that the floor was gone. The wedge-shaped sections of the stone around the tower had begun to slide away from one another—pulling apart like the folds of an iris. "Um, what's happening to your base?"

Shane stepped beside her and shook his head. "No clue. It must have something to do with what your friends were up to."

The shaking stopped as abruptly as it had started.

The panels in the floor had pulled a few feet from one another, revealing gaps that led to a hollow chamber deep below—how deep, it was impossible to tell. The tower in the middle groaned and shuddered, unable to turn any farther. "Whatever that tower is supposed to do, I think it's broken," Abeke said. "The ice must be jamming the mechanism—preventing it from fully opening the floor."

"I hear it down there," Yumaris whispered next to them. "So, so *hungry* . . ."

Abeke didn't have time to consider the old woman's words, because the next moment a mortar shell from

Zerif's fleet crashed into the rock just above their keep. The impact seemed to jolt the entire ledge, nearly knocking Abeke into the abyss below.

She and Shane both ran back into the keep and resumed their positions, just as another cannon fired—striking the keep directly. The impact of the shell knocked the archers backward, raining rubble and shards of ice down from above.

Shane dove on top of Abeke, knocking her clear of a huge chunk of rock that had been blasted loose—rock that would have easily crushed her. Abeke blinked up at Shane, who was staring at her, his expression unreadable. "I . . . can't breathe," she said.

Shane nodded and pulled himself off her. "A simple thanks would suffice." He dusted off his red cloak and picked up his fallen saber.

Abeke sat up, rolling her eyes. When it came to her and Shane, there was nothing simple about it.

"If Zerif keeps up this cannon fire, we won't live to see the landing party," she said.

Shane nodded and helped her to her feet. "I agree."

"King!" Talon shouted. "Check the water! We may be in luck."

Abeke and Shane rushed to the ledge and looked out toward the fleet. White foam sprayed against the choppy waves. Shouts from possessed Greencloaks rang over the water. The largest ship in Zerif's fleet was keeling heavily to one side—nearly capsized. Abeke searched the waters for a reason. Was something attacking the ship from below?

Then she spotted it.

At the helm, three long tentacles with opalescent skin were wrapped around the ship's wheel. The other five were presently engaged in grappling the helmswoman, dragging her away from the steering.

"Mulop!" Abeke said. "He's attacking the fleet."

Another ship sloshed to one side as the first boat rammed into it. There was an earsplitting crack that rang out over even the sounds of birds and waves and cannons—the mast snapping in two. It crashed down onto the deck of the second ship, shattering wood and sending it careening to the side. The cannons that had a moment before been pointing straight at the mountain were now ripped from their stows and flung into the water.

Mulop was single-handedly disarming the entire fleet.

"So much for the cannons!" Shane said, grinning.

But the celebration was cut short before it had even fully begun, for the next moment, Abeke saw the tentacles spasm in pain and grow limp—sliding from the Greencloak and wheel. The octopus's iridescent skin seemed to change before her eyes, turning to a dull, pale color.

"Mulop," she said. "He's been infected."

She thought of Niri sitting underground—the agony the girl must have been experiencing as her spirit animal was ripped from her soul and bonded with Zerif. "Someone should get Niri," she whispered. "She's trapped in that cavern."

"No time . . ." Shane said. "They're here."

Animal snarls and roars filled the air. Zerif's ships had reached the port and an attack party had thrown claw-shaped anchors into the ice. Greencloaks roared as they slid down the ropes and landed at the edge of the island. Animal companions leaped from the ship and joined their sides—snarling and squawking and growling. Abeke watched, openmouthed, trying to count the forces, which seemed to have doubled in size since she last saw them. Zerif must have been adding to his numbers as his fleet traveled from port to port in pursuit of the *Expiator*.

"Wait for my mark," Shane called. "We're going to be driving them to the ledge on the eastern shore, so focus on the group in front. Push them to our left."

Abeke and the Redcloaks held their arrows tight, waiting for his command. Even at this distance, Abeke could see the black stains on their foreheads, marking them as slaves to Zerif. And somewhere in that horde was Zerif himself. She adjusted her grip on the end of her arrow.

"Fire!" Shane cried.

Two dozen arrows soared out from the keep and plunged down to the ice below—lodging into Greencloaks. Screams rang out through the air as six men staggered to their knees, their animal companions faltering beside them. The remaining Greencloak forces veered to one side to avoid the assault.

"Perfect!" Shane said, nocking another arrow. "Keep pushing them in that direction."

Abeke drew another arrow from her quiver and took aim.

"Fire!"

Another volley, this one more successful than the first. A group of fifty or so Greencloaks had splintered off from the main group and was moving closer to the shelf. Abeke and the other archers reloaded and shot again, pushing the invading group to the edge of the ice.

"Release the flue!" Shane cried into the tunnel.

Abeke heard the sound of gears moving deep within the rock and the next moment a burst of searing lava erupted from the side of the mountain. It filled one of the icy trenches, which hissed and steamed, dividing the approaching forces in half.

The lava continued down its path until it reached the fifty Greencloaks huddled on the eastern shelf. Here the trench branched into two smaller streams, which surrounded the group. The ice at this point was thinner, and as soon as the lava made contact, it burned right through and plummeted into the freezing water.

The entire shelf splashed into the ocean. Greencloaks and beasts screamed and splashed, trying to swim to shore in the cold sea.

"Oh-ho!" Yumaris shouted, clapping. "All those nasty greenie-cloaks turned to icicles!"

Abeke glared at the old woman. "If you don't stop talking about my friends and allies like that, there's going to be one *more* icicle floating around out there."

Shane nodded solemnly at Abeke. "We take no pleasure in this," he said, "but the plan worked well."

Abeke only frowned, turning back to the window. Cheers could be heard echoing up from the chambers below. The Redcloaks hadn't defeated Zerif's forces, of course, but they had reduced its numbers by a quarter.

Still, the battle was far from over. Already another wave of Greencloaks had descended from the ships. And the possessed Mulop was already in the water where the Greencloaks had fallen. He was using his tentacles to catch and drag them back to shore—freezing cold, but still alive.

The Redcloaks released another two gates, filling trenches with lava to drive back the incoming forces. The flow created a molten perimeter around the mountain. There was a shout below as another gate opened at the base of the volcano.

This time, instead of lava, there was a flutter of red fabric as a troop of Redcloaks slid down the icy slope, swords in hands. These Redcloaks were not ordinary fighters, for they all possessed traits of the animal companions that they had merged with. They were faster, stronger, fiercer than any human could hope to be. They met the approaching Greencloaks head-on, pushing Zerif's forces back toward the water.

"Fire!" Shane cried, and another volley rained down on the Greencloaks. Abeke crouched beside him, lending her arrows to the cause. Shane and his Redcloaks were fine shots, but none half as good as her. When she let fly an arrow—it always found her mark.

"Nice work, Greencloak!" Talon said, reloading her crossbow. "I think half the fighters in that field have your arrows in them."

Abeke didn't have time to respond to the compliment. She was too busy searching the field for her real prey. And then, in the shifting steam, she saw him—

Zerif.

The man had let his troops charge ahead of him like a coward. Now he was stepping down from the gangplank of his ship, his dark tunic rustling in the wind.

Abeke held her breath, drawing back her arrow. Zerif probably thought he was well out of range, but he couldn't account for the arrows Abeke was using—their obsidian points chiseled to perfection. The ends had been nocked with feathers taken from Essix herself.

The air was cold, but a thin trickle of sweat ran down Abeke's brow.

"Patience," she whispered to herself. She would only have one chance to surprise him.

Zerif reached the shore and marched into the fray—a pair of short swords in his gloved hands. Zerif had seen his share of battles, and even without the power of his Great Beasts, he was a formidable swordsman. He charged toward a Redcloak named Flip who had managed to bound over the main Greencloak forces with a series of impossible, froglike jumps.

Zerif crouched down and slashed one blade quickly through Flip's heel. The Redcloak collapsed, screaming. Zerif stomped on Flip's neck to stifle his cry, before pushing his sword through his heart and silencing him completely.

Abeke wanted to look away from the scene, but she didn't dare blink, for fear of losing her target.

"Patience . . ." she whispered to herself, steam rising from her mouth. The air was blisteringly cold, and she had to fight to keep her aim steady. She could feel the other archers watching her now. Shane had suspended fire, so none of them could distract her from her target. One clean shot and she could end this entire war. "A little closer . . ."

Zerif was almost in range now. He had released his Great Beasts, which slithered and stampeded alongside him—his personal guards, all bonded to him through the parasites: Dinesh the Elephant, Rumfuss the Ram, Gerathon the Serpent, Tellun the Elk, Suka the Polar Bear, Arax the Ram, Halawir the Eagle, and . . .

Abeke caught her breath. "No . . ."

Shane appeared beside her, glancing out the small window. "What's wrong?" he said. "You have a shot, take it."

Abeke blinked, her arrow still nocked in her bow. She adjusted her grip.

"I . . . I can't . . ." Standing in front of Zerif was a sleek yellow beast with deep purple eyes. It was Uraza. *Her* Uraza. The leopard had climbed onto a hunk of fallen ice and was blocking Abeke's shot. If she missed by even an inch, it would go straight through Uraza's neck. The leopard paused, tilting her head up toward the mountain—and then looked directly at Abeke.

Abeke lowered her bow, dropping to the ground. "I can't do it," she said. Her voice was shaking. Her hands slick with sweat. "I can't shoot her. . . ."

She caught the eyes of Talon and Shane, both of whom were looking at her in confusion.

"I'm sorry," she said. She sat up and looked back toward the battlefield—but Uraza and Zerif were both gone.

The ground shook beneath her, violently enough that she had to steady herself against Shane's arm. Chunks of rock and ice fell from the walls around her. There was a huge cracking sound and the entire island shuddered. Redcloaks and Greencloaks alike cried out as the impact threw them all to the ground. A huge crack formed up the side of the volcano wall, showering rubble down on the fighters below.

"What's going on down there?" Talon shouted. "It feels like the mountain's being torn apart from the inside."

Yumaris, who had been huddled in the corner, skittered out from the shadows. "That is the sound of destruction. The end of Erdas." Her face was pale, and for once she sounded completely sane. "Look! Look!" She dragged Abeke and the Redcloaks through the archway to the path overlooking the volcano floor.

The stone panels at the base of the tower had been smashed apart, creating a larger hole. From somewhere deep below, a gargling shriek rang out, curdling the air. Abeke felt a prickly nausea stutter up her spine. She inched closer to the edge of the path for a better look. The broken floor revealed a deep steaming hole that seemed to disappear straight into the heart of Erdas. Streams of hot lava trickled from the edges, bathing it in a dark orange light. And slithering out from that hole was a hideous creature made of slick black tentacles and glowing red eyes.

"The Wyrm," Yumaris whispered. "It's here."

LAST WORDS

WHEN ABEKE WAS YOUNG AND AFRAID OF THE DARK, her mother used to tell her that fear of a thing is more terrible than the sight of it—that the imagination conjures visions worse than anything nature can produce. She would light a torch in their rondavel and explain there was no terror so great it could withstand the light of reality.

But now, staring at the Wyrm, Abeke knew her mother had been wrong. This creature was more disturbing than anything she had ever conceived—and the light of the cavern only served to expose its horror.

The Wyrm was a roiling, slithering nightmare that coated whatever it touched in black ooze. It perched itself on the edge of the chasm from which it had crawled, peering around at the ruins with glowing red eyes. It opened its mouth to reveal row after row of razor-sharp teeth, and screeched.

"Wow," Shane said. "The Hellan carvings didn't quite do it justice."

Yumaris started shaking, backing away from the ledge. "So hungry . . . so hungry . . ."

Battle cries rang out as a few Redcloaks on the lower levels charged the creature, blades drawn. The Wyrm hissed and shot its tendrils out, snatching up the Redcloaks. It snapped their bones like twigs before hurling them away.

"Shane!" It was Talon. Her face was pale. "You need to look outside. The Greencloaks—something's happening to them."

Shane and Abeke pulled themselves away from the sight of the Wyrm and followed Talon back to the window. The icy battlefield was strewn with the bodies of fallen Greencloaks—cut down by arrows and lava and Redcloaks.

But now they were moving. One by one the fallen Greencloaks picked themselves up from the snow. The resurrected army raised their weapons and cried out, their voices as one, in a sort of inhuman roar.

"The Wyrm," Yumaris said, clutching Abeke's arm in her gnarled hands. "It calls to them. Makes them stronger."

"How much stronger?" Shane said, readying his bow.

But he found out soon enough. The reinvigorated Greencloaks charged toward the mountain, cutting past the remaining Redcloaks like they were nothing. Shane called a volley of arrows down on them, but even though most of the arrows found their marks, the horde kept running. They tore through the stone gates with their bare hands and swept into the mountain.

Abeke listened to the shouts and clashing blades as

the battle moved inside the volcano. She thought of Rollan, who was on one of the lower outposts—maybe even within reach of the Wyrm. She closed her eyes, hoping he was smart enough to stay clear of its flailing tentacles.

"How do we stop that thing?" she said.

Shane shook his head. "I have no idea." He had cast aside his bow and drew his saber. The other Redcloak archers drew their own swords. "But we'll die trying."

Abeke followed Shane and his forces down the tunnels—running as fast as her legs could carry her. She had seen the new ferocity of the Greencloaks. She and the others were heading straight into slaughter, but what choice did they have? If just one of them could get close enough to stop the Wyrm, *maybe* they would have a chance at slowing Zerif's forces.

Shane and his Redcloaks had the advantage of animal speed and were pulling ahead of Abeke—leaping from level to level. Abeke cursed her slowness as she slung her bow over her shoulder and clambered down a pile of rubble where the path had fallen away.

"Hollow-girl!" a voice cried beside her.

Abeke dropped down to the path to see Yumaris there. The old woman's mouth hung open in surprise. "There's a message from below. You must follow me. Quickly! Quickly!"

She tried to grab Abeke's hand, but Abeke pulled back. "I don't have time for this," she said. "Shane and the Redcloaks are about to attack the Wyrm before it can reach Zerif."

But Yumaris ignored her. She snatched Abeke's arm

and held it fast. "You must speak to the newling, hollow-girl. Quickly!"

Abeke followed Yumaris through the battle. The closer they came to the hole in the middle of the volcano, the more violent the combat became. Redcloaks fought valiantly against possessed Greencloaks—and the sight of her former comrades fighting tooth and claw against Shane's desperate forces stole her breath away.

Screams and snarls rang out in every direction. Yumaris dragged Abeke through a tunnel that opened into a familiar chamber—to the lava gate where Rollan had been posted with Kirat and the Great Beast summoners.

Howl and Tasha stood at the mouth of the tunnel, fending off approaching Greencloaks, the bulk of whom had focused their efforts on reaching the Wyrm.

"Welcome back," Tasha said as Abeke ran past her and into the cavern. The floor of the cavern was littered with the corpses of snowy terns. Abeke's eyes instantly found Rollan slumped against the wall, Essix on his shoulder.

"You're still alive!" she said, running to him and wrapping him in a hug.

"Barely," Rollan said. He pointed to a bloody gash along his cheek. "Parting gift from one of Zerif's thugs, who managed to scale up through the window. What do you think? Handsome?"

"I'd say you got off easy." She winked. "Meilin will love it."

Rollan's eyes went wide. "Who said anything about Meilin?"

"Enough joking around," Kirat said, rapier in hand. "We have someone who needs to talk to you."

Three of the summoners stepped back from the corner to reveal someone else in the room. A small girl was huddled on the ground, wet and trembling.

Niri stared up at Abeke with shimmering green eyes.

"Niri?" Abeke said, rushing toward her. She knelt down next to the girl, whose face was pale. Niri had red rings under her eyes. It looked like she'd aged ten years in the last three hours. "Mulop," Abeke said. "You lost him."

Niri nodded, her body shaking. "One moment I could feel him . . . and then he was *gone*. . . . It felt like I was ripped in half. . . ." She closed her eyes and tears spilled down her cheeks.

Abeke placed a hand on hers. "I know how it feels." She took a deep breath. "The pain fades, gets duller." This was not exactly true, but she felt like she had to offer some consolation. Abeke looked at Niri's thin legs, which lay motionless on the earth. Her shins and feet were raw and bleeding. "How did you get up here?"

"I pulled myself up from the cavern." She swallowed, massaging her palms, which were also cut. "Dragged myself all the way here. I had to find you." She blinked her eyes, as though trying to stem a fresh tide of tears. "Before Mulop—before *it* happened—I could hear what was happening in Sadre. I know how the trap works—it changes the tides of Erdas. Kovo and the others tried to start the trap in Sadre, but it didn't work. Something went wrong."

Abeke remembered how the rotating tower had stopped abruptly. "It got jammed."

"You have to start the trap—before the Wyrm has a chance to bond with Zerif. Once it finds its host, it will be too powerful."

Abeke straightened up, releasing a steady breath. Having grown up hunting, she knew a thing or two about traps, but this sounded a lot more complicated than what she could pull off with ropes and counter-weights. "How do we spring the trap?"

"They started the trap in Sadre . . . by striking a bell."

"There's no bell in these ruins," Howl said. "King's had us travel through every corridor and passage. Did they tell you where it was?"

"I'm sorry. I don't know any more." Niri shook her head, staring up at them. "But I do know that if you fail, everything is lost."

Rollan scratched his head. "No pressure."

"All right," Kirat said, stepping back. "So our first task is to keep Zerif away from the Wyrm until we can locate this bell. We can set up a perimeter around the edges of the fortress, to keep the Wyrm in the middle of the cavern floor. We don't want it accidentally bringing this entire mountain down on top of us." As he spoke, he drew marks in the dirt with the tip of his sword. "While the Wyrm is distracted, we'll need a second party to sneak into the lower tunnels in search of the bell." He turned to Howl. "I'm guessing you have a good nose. Do you think you could lead the search?"

Howl gave a lupine grin. "Try and stop me."

"Good," Kirat continued. "Tasha should go with you. She can summon Ninani to search places that are out of reach or might be hidden from the ground."

Abeke was impressed. Kirat really did sound like his uncle. And more important, he had a plan.

Rollan must have read her mind. "He's been like this since you left. I'd be annoyed if it weren't for the fact that I know Tarik would approve." He shrugged. "Besides, it's nice to have someone else to blame when things go wrong."

"Let's not talk about things going wrong," Abeke said.

A cry broke out from the tunnel as Howl and Tasha were knocked backward by a snarling streak of yellow. The two screamed in pain, clutching their arms. Blood seeped from long claw marks where they had been slashed through their cloaks.

Standing above them was a sleek creature with violet eyes.

23

LOSS

ABEKE STARED AT THE BEAST, HER HEART RACING. "Uraza?" she said. It was the closest she'd been to her spirit animal since losing her on the rocky shores of Zourtzi.

The Great Beast stalked closer to Abeke, licking her white fangs. The parasite beneath her leopard brow was pulsing and black, wriggling and twisting beneath the flesh. The rims of Uraza's eyes were bloodshot and dark. She looked like a changed creature.

Rollan and the others drew their blades.

"Weapons down!" Abeke shouted. "No one hurts her."

She lowered her own bow, keeping her eyes fixed on Uraza's. "I don't know what Zerif's done to you, but I *know* you, Uraza." Her voice was shaking. "Deep down, I know you don't want to hurt—"

Uraza roared, leaping straight at her, claws raised—pouncing to kill.

"No!" Abeke screamed, stumbling backward.

She registered a flash of red fabric and Uraza's body suddenly hurtled to one side—veering off course and smashing against the cavern wall. The beast roared and snapped at the thing that had prevented her from killing Abeke.

Rollan rushed to Abeke's side, helping her up.

Abeke could only stare at the swirling red cape rolling across the ground, the figure fighting to subdue Uraza. One of the Redcloaks had leaped to save her. She caught a glint of yellow eyes behind a plain white mask as her rescuer drew his saber.

"Shane," she whispered.

Even with his heightened speed, Shane was too slow. Uraza bit down on his side, and Shane cried out in agony, dropping his sword. The Great Beast drew him off the ground and shook him back and forth, driving her teeth deeper into his flesh.

Abeke had hunted with Uraza countless times. She'd seen her do similar things to finish off wounded prey. But now the prey was *Shane*.

"Let him go!" Abeke scrambled across the dirt and grabbed her bow. This time she did not hesitate. She nocked an arrow and aimed it at Uraza.

The arrow plunged straight through Uraza's leg.

The Great Leopard snarled and stumbled back, releasing Shane, who fell to the ground with a dull thud.

Uraza gave a gargling wheeze, as if struggling for air. Blood ran freely from her wound. She roared at Abeke and then—in a flash of bright light—vanished from her spot, leaving only a red stain on the cavern floor. She had been summoned into passive state by her new master.

"Shane!" Abeke ran to the boy, falling to her knees.

Shane moaned in pain. Dark blood soaked his side. His skin was pale and covered with perspiration.

"Just keep breathing," she said, taking his head in her hands. "Keep breathing...."

Shane lolled his head toward her, opening his yellow eyes. "I . . . saw Uraza running toward the tunnel and I was afraid she might . . . hurt you." He flinched, clenching his jaw tight as he gave a painful cough. When he opened his mouth again, there was blood on his lips.

"I . . . I'm sorry, Abeke." His voice was so weak she could barely hear it over the sounds of battle echoing up from the tunnels below. "I'm sorry for everything." He winced, giving another violent cough.

He did not move again.

"Not you. . . . Not you. . . ." Abeke clutched the boy's lifeless body in her arms, pulling him close to her chest. He had given his life trying to win her forgiveness. If she had only told him before how she felt, what he meant to her, he might still be alive.

Abeke clenched her eyes shut, letting the tears spill down her face. Tarik, the Greencloaks, Uraza, Shane . . . It was all too much loss. Too much destruction. Her legs felt numb beneath her. Her entire body shook as she released a rasping sob.

She became aware of new people charging into the chamber. There were shouts, and the clashing of swords, and animal roars—a short scuffle that seemed to end as soon as it had begun. Abeke wiped her eyes and looked up to see three dozen of Zerif's Greencloaks lining the wall of the cavern, each with swords at the necks of her friends. If there had been a fight, it was a quick one—normal children were no match for trained Greencloaks.

Her eyes found a tall figure wearing a dark tunic, who was watching her with an amused expression.

"Zerif," she said, releasing her grip on Shane's body.

"Poor little Abeke," the man said, stepping close to her. "How far you've fallen." His tunic was torn, revealing the intersecting tattoos of his stolen Great Beasts—including the shape of Uraza. "I remember when I first found you: half-feral, fresh from hunting alone in the savannah, despite your father's disapproval. You were meek and obedient at the time, but I could sense—deep down—that you had the instincts of a killer."

Zerif's lip curled in disgust. "Now look at you. A whimpering child, crying over the corpse of the boy who betrayed you. I had such high hopes for you once. You traded unlimited power for a shabby green cloak." He shrugged. "Then again, maybe I should thank you. If Kovo *had* succeeded, then I might not be here right now. Commander of eight Great Beasts—oops, make that nine!" He smiled at Niri, who was still lying defenseless in the corner. "Mulop says hello." He held out his palm to reveal a tattoo of an octopus.

"If it's all the same to you," Rollan said, "I'd rather you just kill us. Anything is better than listening to you gloat."

"Now, now, Rollan." Zerif wagged a finger. "Don't be a sore loser. Besides, I wouldn't dream of killing you . . . *yet*." He gave a poisonous smile. He pointed to the boy's chest, where the mark of Essix was visible beneath a tear in his shirt. "You have something I want. Besides, you

Greencloak brats should be alive to witness your defeat firsthand."

Abeke was pulled to her feet by a Southern Zhonghese girl.

"Abeke, meet Raisha," Zerif said cheerfully. "I don't believe you two have been introduced. Raisha was a wonderful assistant when I first began this little undertaking. She helped me gather so many of the Great Beasts. And then, when she herself summoned Gerathon the Serpent, Raisha became an even greater help."

Raisha's eyes were dark and expressionless. The girl's skin was so pale it was almost translucent, and her hair had grown brittle and thin. Abeke tried to pull herself free, but Raisha's grip was inhumanly strong. And it made sense. There was hardly anything human about her anymore.

"We'll just hang on to those," Zerif hissed as Raisha removed Abeke's bow and quiver, heaving them around her own shoulder.

Abeke and Rollan and the other children were led through the tunnels into the central chamber of the volcano. The half-opened floor of the ruins glowed orange from the streams of fresh magma pouring into the chasm. The frozen tower in the middle of the volcano had begun to thaw in the heat, leaking streams of water that ran down through the cracks and fizzled into clouds of sulfuric steam.

The perimeter of the chamber was lined with Redcloaks, all of whom were also being held at swordpoint by Zerif's thralls. And in the middle of the crag, perched on the edge of a shard of rock, was the Wyrm.

"Whoa," Rollan muttered. "That thing's even uglier up close—*unngff*!" He grimaced as the Greencloak holding him twisted his arm.

"Ugly?" Zerif said, turning around. "I think it's rather beautiful." He placed his hands behind his back, staring at the twitching beast before them. "A creature of raw and infinite power—power that will soon be mine."

Abeke stared at the Wyrm, which was watching Zerif with its glowing eyes. She had no idea whether the creature could understand what Zerif was saying or if it cared. The Wyrm's expression was inscrutable, but she had the uncanny feeling that it was hungry.

"You really think you can control that thing?" she said.

Zerif gave a wary chuckle. "You ask this of the man who commands two hundred Greencloaks and a battalion of Great Beasts? The man who devastated the fallen King Shane and his ridiculous Redcloaks." He turned back to the waiting Wyrm. "This creature understands the natural order of Erdas—it will submit to one more powerful than itself. And if it resists, I have ways to change its mind." He slid a hand into his haversack and removed a small glass vial. Inside was a tiny black parasite—the same sort of parasite he had used to possess Uraza and the other Great Beasts. The same parasite that controlled his Greencloak army.

Abeke watched him uncork the vial and walk toward the Wyrm. "Easy now," he said, holding the bottle out in front of him. "This won't hurt a bit. . . ."

The Wyrm did not recoil or show any signs of struggle. Instead it opened its mouth and gave a sort of chirping shriek. At once, the Greencloaks closest to Zerif marched toward him and grabbed the man by the arms, pinning him to one spot.

"Stop!" Zerif cried out in surprise. "I command you to release me!"

But the Greencloaks held him fast.

Zerif's vial fell to the ground, shattering against the rock. The parasite, now freed, wriggled its way across the stone until it reached the Wyrm.

The huge creature extended one of its oozing black tentacles. With a touch, the parasite's writhing shape melted away—their shining black hides melding into one.

"The parasites . . ." Abeke said. "They're *part of* the Wyrm." She looked around at the blank expressions of the infected Greencloaks and Great Beasts, and thought she understood what was happening. All of them, human and animal alike, were being controlled by the Wyrm—they had a fraction of the Wyrm inside their minds.

The Wyrm shrieked again, and the Greencloaks holding Zerif pulled him toward the creature's open mouth.

"This is not what was supposed to happen!" Zerif screamed, kicking out his legs. "I command you! Let *go!*" He pulled and thrashed, trying to get free, but the possessed Greencloaks dragged him ever closer.

Abeke watched in horror, finally understanding.

Zerif was never the hunter, she realized. *He was the prey.*

The Wyrm hissed as its every tentacle descended upon Zerif—plunging right into his flesh.

"*Noooooo!*" the man screamed. Thin black tendrils snaked beneath his skin, flooding his body with viscous ooze. As this happened, the Wyrm itself became smaller—it was as though the creature was pouring itself into his veins.

Abeke shut her eyes, unable to watch. She wished her hands were free so she could cover her ears to block out Zerif's cries.

He was evil. He deserved to die. But no living creature deserved *this*.

A moment later, the screaming stopped. Abeke opened her eyes again to find that the Wyrm was no longer there.

Instead there was only Zerif. The man had been released by the Greencloaks and now lay collapsed on the ground, gasping and wheezing. He slowly pulled himself upright. For a moment Zerif just stood there, teetering under his own weight, his dark eyes shining against the red light.

Then he spoke.

"At lassstttt," he said in a deep, inhuman voice—one that seemed to reverberate through his every pore, *"I am fully borrrnnnn."*

SLAVE AND MASTER

ABEKE STARED AT ZERIF...OR RATHER THE THING THAT had been Zerif just a moment before.

His eyes were completely dark—shining pools of ooze that swirled and shifted unnaturally. His skin was a dull gray, lined with twitching veins that pulsed and shifted as he breathed. He was not a man anymore. He was a shell.

Abeke wanted to scream, to run away from him. But Raisha held her fast to her spot, her scaly hands digging deep into Abeke's flesh.

"What did you do to Zerif?" Abeke said to the Thing standing before her.

The Thing that had been Zerif tilted its head, an almost curious expression on its ghastly face.

"*Whatt I diddd?*" Its words were garbled, as though it were still learning how to use its new human mouth. "*Whatt I diddd?*"

The Thing stretched out its hand toward one of the nearest Redcloaks—a woman named Shadow. Thin black tentacles shot out of its fingertips and wrapped around the woman's neck. Shadow let out a cry as she was lifted clear off the ground. Abeke watched in horror as her skin went from brown to gray to white. Even her dark hair lost its color. It was as though the Thing were sucking the very life from her. With a final twitch, the woman's body went limp.

The Thing jerked its hand and flung Shadow's lifeless body into the gaping chasm behind it.

"*Aaahhhh,*" the Thing sighed as its tentacles withdrew back into its hand. It licked its teeth, which were stained black.

"Zerif, can you hear me?" Abeke shouted, hoping desperately that he could. "You have to resist the Wyrm's power—you have to fight back before it consumes you!"

"*Conssssummmme . . .*" the Thing said. "*Yesssssss.*" It turned its eyes toward something just behind Abeke. It flicked out a tongue, as if tasting the air. A hungry smile spread across its black lips. "*Aaaahhhhh . . .*"

Abeke craned her neck to see that the Thing was looking straight at Rollan. The boy stared right back at it, his eyes burning with hate. "Just try it, you ugly sack of—"

Before he could even finish speaking, the Thing had lashed out at Rollan with its tentacles—lifting him clear off the ground.

"No!" Abeke screamed, pulling against Raisha's grip. The girl held her fast.

Rollan screamed, his body contorting in pain. With a desperate roar, he ripped his left arm free of its oozing binds and touched the tattoo on his chest. In a flash, Essix was above him, beating her wings.

"Essix, fly away!" Rollan screamed. "Don't let it take you!"

The gyrfalcon didn't listen. She screeched, swooping straight at Rollan's attacker with her talons spread.

The Thing that had been Zerif was ready. It raised its other hand and quickly caught Essix in its tendrils—holding them both aloft over the gaping pit.

Abeke watched, trembling, as Rollan and his Great Beast screamed in pain—their eyes growing dimmer as the Thing sucked the very life from them. In another minute, they would both be dead. She had to *do* something!

She scanned the cavern and saw Niri. The girl had been dragged through the tunnels by one of the Greencloaks. Niri had told her that they had to find some sort of bell—but there was no bell—and even if they could find it, it was already too late.

Rollan screamed again. Abeke clenched her eyes shut, feeling the full weight of her failure. She had fought for so long, and for what? Everything she touched turned to destruction. Soon even these ruins would crumble around her.

She opened her eyes and saw that the ground beneath her feet was wet. Thin streams of water cascaded down from the ice into the middle of the ruins. She blinked, peering up the length of the tower.

A small circle of red sky was still visible overhead. The top of the tower glinted against the setting sun as the final bits of ice melted away, revealing an open platform just beneath the stone cornice. Hanging from the ancient rafters was something dark and heavy and made of iron—

A bell.

Abeke stared up at the bell, catching her breath. It had been right in front of them the whole time. Only now it was too late. Even if ringing the bell could somehow help, she was a hundred feet beneath it with only seconds to spare.

"Sssooo sssweet," the Thing snarled, raising its prey higher over its head. Rollan screamed out again, but his voice sounded fainter, like the last drops of life were being sucked from him. His eyes met Abeke's. He moved his lips, but no words came out. She knew that she was seeing her friend for the last time. This was the end.

Abeke didn't have time to consider the odds. She didn't have time to consider her pain. She had to act. With a desperate cry, she swung her head backward, slamming her skull into Raisha's jaw. Her captor screamed and staggered backward, as much out of surprise as pain. Abeke spun around and snatched the bow and quiver from Raisha's shoulder.

Raisha shrieked, trying to grab her lost prisoner. Abeke dove clear of her grasp and rolled across the ground. She sprang to her feet with her bow raised—an arrow pointed directly at the Thing. "Let them go!" she said, her obsidian arrowhead glinting in the magma's warm light. She could feel the others in the chamber watching her, confused, terrified.

The Thing that had been Zerif seemed to pause a moment, keeping Rollan and Essix both hanging in the air, somewhere between life and death. *"It would threaten meeee?"* It stretched its mouth into a rictus grin.

"The arrow's not for you," Abeke said. And quick as a flash, she raised her bow over her head and let fly.

THE BURNING TIDE

A BEKE'S ARROW ARCED THROUGH THE AIR FOR WHAT felt like an eternity. Finally it sliced up through the high bannister railing and struck the edge of the bell with a light *ting!*

The sound was barely a whisper, but it echoed through the whole cavern. Everyone around Abeke seemed to be holding their collective breath, waiting to see what would happen next. Even the Thing dropped its prey and was watching the bell.

And when Abeke saw its face, she could tell that it was nervous. *"It knowssss this..."* it hissed. *"Turningggg..."*

The ringing of the bell finally gave way to another sound—a deep rumbling that shook the entire mountain. The tower in the middle of the ruins trembled and then shifted, slowly rotating on its axis. Rubble and ice fell from the walls of the volcano, crashing to the cavern floor around Abeke. There was a ripping sound as part of the bottom wall broke loose—letting a flood of cold water gush in from the ocean outside.

The biggest change, however, was in the hole. The panels of the cavern floor retreated into the walls of the mountain, revealing a huge chasm that went straight down into the heart of Erdas. Redcloaks and Greencloaks alike scrambled to find stable ground around the perimeter. The Thing had also moved, stranding itself on the front steps of the bell tower, which was now surrounded by yawning darkness on all sides.

The bell tower continued rotating. Its foundation seemed to go down as far as the chasm. Stone buttresses secured the lower tower to the inside walls of the tunnel, and as these moved, giant cracks appeared in the hole. Bubbling magma from deep within the earth spewed out, filling the hole to the very brim. The magma churned and frothed—creating a hissing whirlpool around the spinning tower.

As the tower turned, Abeke felt a sort of queasy shift in the air, like her stomach was folding inside out. The hair on the back of her neck stood on end, and she feared her teeth were going to crack. She wasn't the only one experiencing strange symptoms. Yumaris and the Redcloaks were all clutching their heads in agony, as if they were being ripped apart from the inside. Zerif's Greencloaks had dropped to the ground and were snarling and shrieking and snorting in furious confusion. Some tried to dig into the rock with their hands. Others were climbing the walls. Their spirit animals staggered around, bumping into one another as though confused about where they were.

The only ones unaffected by the tower seemed to be Abeke and the other kids who had *lost* their spirit animals. They all remained standing, watching the chaos around them.

"What's happening to my brother?" Dawson Trunswick said, backing away from Worthy. Devin was writhing on the cavern floor, clutching his head. "What did you do?"

Abeke swallowed, shaking her head. "I have no idea."

There are some moments that seem to be almost infinite.

When Rollan saw Abeke's arrow soar up toward the sky and strike the bell, he felt as though it was the death knell of his own existence. The Wyrm creature had sucked him dry, and all that was left for him to do was let go and slip into death. But then something strange happened. That bell's chime continued to ring and ring and ring. It rang so loud that the entire world around him began to shake and blur. He felt a prickling nausea sweep through his entire body and the next thing he knew, he was floating high in the air, staring down at his own body, which lay at the foot of the stone tower.

This is what people must mean by an out-of-body experience, he thought. Rollan flapped his wings, watching as his thin body lurched forward, blinking in confusion, darting its head all around. The sight was so strange that it took Rollan a second to realize that he was *flapping his wings*.

Rollan opened his mouth to let out a cry, but all that came was a raspy *squawk!* The boy on the ground darted his head up and stared at Rollan—looking truly bewildered.

And that's when the true realization came over him. He wasn't Rollan from Concorba. He was a bird. And not just any bird . . . He was *Essix* . . . or rather, his mind was *inside* Essix's body.

Rollan let out another bewildered squawk and rose up higher into the air.

All he could think to do was fly higher and higher until he burst from the mouth of the volcano. He stretched out his wings and let the cold air beat against his face.

For the first time in his life, he felt truly *free*.

Deep underground, on the other side of Erdas, Meilin felt a rumbling beneath her as the snare in the middle of the fallen city began to turn once more. She stumbled to one side and in the space of a shuddering heartbeat, she found herself staring out from a different pair of eyes—dark, animal eyes pressed into the muzzle of a soft, round face. She stared at her paws, black fur stained red with blood from the battle against the Wyrm.

She blinked, looking out at the host of wounded Sadrean soldiers in the Fallen City. Every face she saw filled her with an aching pang. She felt an overwhelming desire to care for every person suffering—to make each of them whole again.

She padded onto the battlefield and began to help.

For Conor, it was like waking from a terrible dream. Dreams were something Conor was good at—and more than once he had experienced dreams that showed him his own future. But all of those were nothing compared to this. He had been trapped inside his own body for so long, unable to fight the power of the parasite.

But then he opened his eyes and knew—knew instantly—that something had shifted in Erdas. The fever was gone. The wriggling parasite no longer burrowing into his flesh. The Wyrm's voice no longer hissing in his mind.

The shores of the Sulfur Sea had drawn back, as if pulled away from the city by some invisible force. Conor drew himself up and limped over to a pool of dark water left in the sand. He bowed his head, lapping at the pool with his pink tongue. Then he stood upright and stared into his reflection. Blue eyes as deep as the sky. It was the face of Briggan.

Abeke stared at the cavern, which was now echoing with the sounds of hundreds of confused Greencloaks and their even more confused spirit animals. But as she watched them, she began to see how they were behaving—the humans acting like beasts, and the beasts like humans.

Everyone except Abeke and the other children who had lost their spirit animals.

"The snare," she said. "It's somehow reversed the connection between humans and their animal companions."

The words sounded ludicrous coming out of her

mouth, but her eyes told a different story. She stared up at the tower, which was still turning, though more slowly now. The swirling lava bubbled and hissed around it, creating a fiery whirlpool. "Look at the tides!" called the girl Cordalles, pointing at a gaping hole in the rock.

Abeke looked outside and saw that the ocean was churning, swelling up into huge waves that swirled in the same direction as the lava. Even the spilled water from the icy tower was cutting an arc across the ground, moving on its own.

Abeke looked back toward the tower—at the Thing that was Zerif. The figure remained standing but was staring around at the cavern with a confused expression, inching back from the swirling lava at his feet. And when Abeke saw his eyes, she caught a slight flash of hazel. The same eyes she had first seen in her village in Nilo.

"Zerif!" she shouted. Abeke still had her bow and quiver. She wanted to shoot every arrow she had at the man—but one look at his face and she knew that he was just as much a victim of the Wyrm as anyone. She didn't need revenge. She needed to stop the Wyrm. "Zerif!" she called more loudly.

The man fixed his bloodshot gaze on her. "What . . . what have you done to me?" he said, his voice shaking. "What's happening?"

"There's no time to explain," Abeke said, racing to the edge of the lava pool. There was a groaning crunch as a huge crack ran up the length of the tower, which had begun to slow its rotation. The strain of Erdas was too much for the snare. "The bell has put you in control of the Wyrm," she said. "You have one chance to stop it."

"Stop it . . . ?" he said blankly. Zerif glanced down at his gray hands, which were still pulsing with the black veins of the Wyrm.

Cracks spread up the volcano walls, raining down rubble. Abeke shielded her face as huge chunks of stone fell around her.

"The tower won't last much longer!" she screamed. "Zerif, *please!*" The idea that she was pleading with *Zerif* of all people to stop the Wyrm was beyond comprehension. But she had no choice.

What was a hero but someone who had chosen *one time* to do the right thing? Shane had saved Abeke from Uraza. Kovo had built the snare.

Could Zerif kill the Wyrm?

"I can't force you to do anything," she said. "Either you kill the Wyrm now, or you will spend the rest of your life enslaved to it."

The stone tower cracked in half, falling into the molten pool, which swallowed it whole. The whirling lava stopped churning and started to drain back into the earth. Abeke could feel a static prickle in the air as Erdas pushed back against the turning. The swirls of water cutting across the stone floor exploded into a scatter of droplets.

"There's no time!" Abeke screamed.

All around her, the Greencloaks and spirit animals were calming down—their minds returning to their rightful bodies. The Redcloaks had begun to stir. Zerif staggered to one side, doubling over in pain. When he looked up at her again, one of his eyes had turned to black. "*Sssstopp meeeee?*" he hissed in the voice of the Wyrm.

"Fight back, Zerif!" Abeke cried.

Zerif planted a hand against the rumbling tower, the other pressed to his temple. "Get out of my head!" he roared. His one human eye was clenched shut, streaming tears. She could see him fighting the Wyrm for control.

"Do it!" she begged.

Zerif screamed like a man being torn in two. With a desperate cry, he pushed himself away from the tower and staggered toward the lava, leaping from the edge of the rock—

The moment his feet left the ground, his body contorted and spun around. The Wyrm took control of his body once more. Black tendrils shot outward, flailing in the air as it plummeted down into the chasm and the churning lava.

Abeke scrambled to the edge and watched as the Thing that was Zerif disappeared beneath the fiery surface of the magma.

She sat back, breathing hard. Abeke stared at the lava, still terrified that the creature might somehow pull itself free. That it had somehow survived.

But then she heard the voices behind her. Not just one, not just a dozen, but *hundreds* of voices. Men and women, muttering to one another in bewildered tones. Abeke turned around to see Greencloaks, many of them kneeling on the floor of the cavern, some in tears. Those who could walk had rushed to the sides of the Redcloaks to help them. The Greencloaks' faces were battered and bleeding from the fight, but their eyes—their eyes showed the clear glint of humanity.

The Wyrm was truly gone.

HUNTER AND PREY

ABEKE TIGHTENED HER HAND AROUND THE GRIP OF her bow. It was a crude weapon—she had carved it from the soft limb of a baobab tree. Usually, baobab would be terrible for bows, with not enough tension in the string. But this baobab, like every tree in Erdas, was changed now, its roots infused with the power of the revived Evertree. She could feel *life* coursing through the pores of the bow's grain, connecting with her hand, her spirit.

Abeke ducked down, hearing a rustling in the bushes below. She was in the hot jungles of Stetriol. Sweat beaded her brow. The jungle floor was thick with vines and brush, and so she had been forced to make her way through the canopy of trees, carefully climbing from limb to limb. She had been living like this for weeks, barely eating or sleeping.

She was a hunter. And she would have her prey.

Below her, the jungle wildlife ticked and croaked—oblivious to her presence. It had been months since the destruction of the Wyrm at the hands of Kovo's ancient snare. For one brief moment, all of Erdas had been transformed. Spirit bonds across the world were reversed. Seas had drawn back from the shores. Storms had raged in the sky. The Wyrm, housed inside Zerif's body, had been plunged into the burning whirlpool in the center of Erdas. And then, just like that, everything had returned to normal.

But of course, everything *wasn't* normal. The Wyrm had left one final gift to the world it tried to destroy. The power that fueled the Wyrm was washed into the tides. Every spring began to bubble with the same power that fueled the bond between humans and beasts. Every blade of grass and flower and tree became a smaller version of the Evertree.

The world was connected in new ways. Abeke didn't know what this meant for Erdas. She hoped it was good.

But amid that new life, there was still pain.

Abeke recalled the moments after the death of the Wyrm. A stillness had settled over the molten ruins in the Frozen Sea as the humans and beasts who had been possessed by the Wyrm's parasites recovered—blinking as if waking from a slumberless dream.

Abeke could still hear the haunting wails of grief that rang out inside the volcano as the Greencloaks regained their minds and recalled the horrific things they had done while under Zerif's control.

They were free of Zerif perhaps, but they would forever be captive to their own guilt.

Mulop, again restored to Niri, had been able to speak

with Kovo underground, and arranged a reunion. Abeke and Rollan managed to get passage to Eura, where they met Conor and Meilin, who had emerged safely from the tunnels of Sadre. Takoda was with them, too, his hand intertwined with a pale girl named Xanthe's.

For the first time in centuries, the Sadreans and the people of Erdas met and communed with one another. This was important, because it would take every living soul to repair the damage Zerif and the Wyrm had done. Every port Abeke and Rollan passed, they saw firsthand the destruction that the Greencloaks had wrought.

When Abeke finally saw Conor and Briggan waiting for them at the shore, she leaped clear off the edge of her ship onto the decks and sprinted toward him at a full run.

Conor, like the other Greencloaks, had recovered from his parasite infection. But just like them, he was haunted by his actions while under the Wyrm's control. All traces of the youthful shepherd had disappeared, leaving him looking older, more wary. And just like the Greencloaks, he now had a thin, colorless scar on his forehead, only visible in certain light.

Rollan and Meilin were surprisingly awkward upon seeing each other again. Rollan, usually quick with a joke, said almost nothing, while Meilin rambled on with uncharacteristic speed. Neither made eye contact, or even tried to approach the other. It wasn't until Jhi padded next to Meilin and shoved her straight into Rollan—forcing them into an accidental hug—that things began to turn back to normal.

They were a family restored—all of them together once more.

All but one.

Beyond the safety of her friends, Abeke had one all-consuming concern: What had happened to the Great Beasts that had been bonded with Zerif?

This was a question no one could answer. Not even Mulop, with his powers, had been able to sense Uraza's presence. Some people speculated the Great Beasts had died when Zerif hurled himself into the lava. Others said that they had been released into the burning currents beneath Erdas and spread to a thousand shores.

But soon enough, reports began to arrive of Great Beasts being spotted all across the world.

A gallant elk emerged from the mists of Northern Amaya one morning, appearing to a tribe of nomadic hunters. The elk walked unworriedly through their encampment as the hunters gaped on, until it had reached their young healer.

In Southern Zhong, a crowded marketplace erupted into chaos one steamy evening as an enormous elephant appeared from the jungle, wearing silks across its back and bracelets on its tusks. A small grinning girl sat astride it, waving to the crowd.

In Eura, a band of pirates was arrested when their ship crashed near a port city. They claimed an eagle had ripped their sails to shreds just as they tried to seize a merchant vessel. After leaving a steaming present on the hull of their pirate ship, it landed on the arm of a girl with a dignified squawk.

One by one, every Great Beast reappeared—
Every beast but one.

Abeke didn't know why Uraza remained hidden. Soon after the death of the Wyrm, the spot on her arm where Uraza's tattoo *would* be began to tingle, which she took as proof that Uraza was out there somewhere. But for some reason, the Great Leopard had not tried to find her.

Then again, maybe Abeke already knew why. Every night as she went to sleep, her dreams returned to the horror of a possessed Uraza killing Shane—her sharp teeth locked around his lifeless body. And then she felt the wrenching pain of letting fly her own arrow straight into her spirit animal's side.

At first, when Abeke had told her friends that she needed to leave in search of Uraza, they had tried to come with her. But she explained that she needed to do this alone. For six months, the huntress had kept her ear to the ground, searching for rumors of the great Uraza. The rumors had taken her to nearly every continent, but everywhere she went, she found nothing.

Now, at last, her search had brought her to Stetriol. The last place on Erdas. The jungles here were dangerous. Beasts that had once been enslaved by the Bile lurked in the untamed wilds—their anger at humans meant that more than a few of them would be happy to eat her if she wasn't careful. But she couldn't turn back. She knew she was close. She *had* to be close.

Her arm seemed to sense the spirit bond between her and Uraza. The tingling sensation grew, until she could almost feel it vibrating as she came closer to her prey. Abeke wanted to call out, to let Uraza know she was there, but she was afraid to frighten her off.

There was a rustling in the jungle beneath her. Abeke turned around and saw something watching her from the shadows. Something with flashing purple eyes. The eyes held her gaze for a moment, and then a sleek golden leopard poured out from between the leaves.

Not since that first day in Okaihee had the sight of her spirit animal filled Abeke with such unrestrained joy. She nearly burst into tears right there.

Instead, Abeke just grinned, leaping down from the trees.

Uraza stepped forward, watching her tentatively. Abeke had expected the leopard to be angry with her, perhaps even fearful. Instead, she was surprised to see shame in Uraza's violet eyes.

Abeke extended a slow, shaking hand outward. Just as slowly, the leopard brought her face forward—and nuzzled into her palm.

With that touch, everything was right again. Joy flooded through Abeke like rain on a parched savannah. Suddenly she *was* crying, harder than she had let herself cry in a long while.

Apologies would come with time. Apologies and forgiveness. For now, Abeke's body was electric with relief. Unsure what to do with this sudden rush of energy, she *whooped* into the trees.

Uraza purred heavily, slinking away. Her eyes flashed with a playful gleam. Abeke suspected that her spirit animal had some ideas for how to celebrate their reunion. In seconds, the leopard had disappeared into the brush.

Abeke's face split into a smile as she followed Uraza into the trees.

The hunt was on.

Jonathan Auxier writes strange stories for strange children—including *Peter Nimble and His Fantastic Eyes, The Night Gardener,* and *Sophie Quire and the Last Storyguard*. Raised in Canada, Jonathan now lives in Pittsburgh with his wife and family.

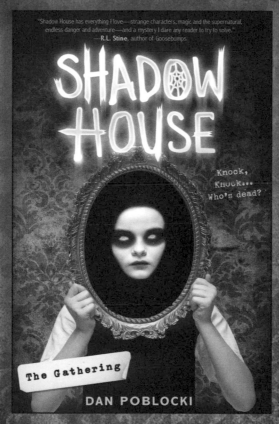